If Abigail O'Con[nor] [...] [...] [...]s Titus feel so wretched when another man pays attention to her?

Titus grabbed a cup of coffee from a nearby store while he waited for Abigail. He passed some time talking with the neighborhood men, who groused about no work and poor living conditions. Titus barely tolerated the strong coffee but managed to get it down just the same. He had to agree the Irish neighborhood conditions were worse than what he and his family had to endure.

Of course, with people like Abigail O'Connor to help them. . .

He ignored the dip of his heart with the thought of her. His thoughts turned smug. *Abigail O'Connor and her charity work. Just like her father trying to salve his conscience by hiring me, most likely she, too, has something to hide.*

He would find out their weakness. It might take some time, but if he remained patient, they would crumble. He'd see to that.

After a while, he went back to the carriage and waited in his seat. The front doors finally creaked open, and his head jerked up.

"Thank you, again, Abigail, for your fine help today. I can see the children have immediately taken to you," the man beside her was saying. Abigail smiled at him and waved good-bye. The sight of the man standing beside her brought an uncomfortable twist to Titus's gut. He jumped from his carriage seat and went over to escort her.

DIANN HUNT resides in Indiana with her husband. They have two grown children and four grand-daughters whom they love to spoil ad nauseum. Through her stories, Diann hopes to encourage readers with the message of God's love and constancy in an ever-shifting world. Visit her website at www.diannhunt.com

Books by Diann Hunt

HEARTSONG PRESENTS
HP507—Trunk of Surprises
HP603—A Whale of a Marriage

Very Very Good

Diann Hunt

AUTHOR

Basket of Secrets

TITLE

DATE DUE	BORROWER'S NAME

A note from the Author:
I love to hear from my readers! You may correspond
with me by writing:

Diann Hunt
Author Relations
PO Box 719
Uhrichsville, OH 44683

ISBN 1-59310-445-6

BASKET OF SECRETS

*Our mission is to publish and distribute inspirational products offer-
ing exceptional value and biblical encouragement to the masses.*

All scripture quotations are taken from the King James Version of the
Bible.

PRINTED IN THE U.S.A.

Or check out our Web site at www.heartsongpresents.com

one

Abigail O'Connor watched as the dark carriage rattled toward the train station, taking away the only man she'd ever loved. Her chance for happiness had rushed in like the waters of Lake Michigan to the Chicago shorelines, then seemed to flee like an ebbing tide.

"Abigail, come down and eat something," her mother encouraged from the stairwell.

Wiping away the last tear, the twenty-six-year-old dropped the lace curtain from her window, muting the afternoon sun to dull shadows in her bedroom. She walked to the washstand. The cool splash of water against her face erased the tears but still left behind the stain upon her heart. A towel lay nearby. She picked up the soft cloth and dried her skin with it, all the while struggling to find relief from the pain that plagued her.

With reluctance, she stepped in front of the looking glass. One glance and she pulled in a sharp breath. Crying did little good for her appearance. Her fingers probed gently around the puffy area of her eyes.

"How could you do this to me, Jonathan?" Her words, a mixture of anger and sorrow, echoed within the confines of her room. Once more, she dabbed the towel on her face with more force than necessary, stinging her delicate skin. Frustrated, she turned and threw the towel on her bed. She thought a moment, then lifted her chin. "Well, if that's what you want, Jonathan Clark, go back east. Build a new life for yourself. I'll get along fine without you." She gulped back a fresh wave of tears.

The dress hanging on a peg on the wall caught her attention. A dress designed by her best friend, Sophia Hill.

Sophia and Clayton Hill. If only Abigail could find happiness with someone as they had found in one another. She couldn't imagine Clayton and Sophia would soon celebrate their first anniversary. Almost a year since the fire.

Almost a year since Jonathan had walked into her life and stolen her heart.

She remembered the day well. She had gone to the Thread Bearer to discuss the Christmas ball with Sophia. Jonathan had arrived shortly after to help Sophia with her ledger books. Catching the fancy of the handsome bookkeeper, Abigail had left with a promise of an escort to the ball. They had been a couple since that time. Until a week ago. When he told her he took another position. Back east. He couldn't pass it up, he had said.

Obviously, he didn't love her. She'd have to move on with her life. But how?

Abigail sighed and fell onto the bed. She sank into the thick blankets and plump pillows. Their comfort did little to ease her misery. Why did Jonathan feel the need for a bigger, better job back east? Despite her anger, she felt a twinge of understanding. He no doubt wanted to go home. She couldn't blame him for that. She wanted to stay near family, too. But would she have given up family for him? Her back stiffened. Without a doubt, she would have given up everything for him. She felt almost sure she would have.

Almost.

Rising to her feet, she brushed down the front and sides of her skirt with her hands, smoothing out wrinkles. She would not wallow in self-pity one moment longer. Quickly, she returned to the looking glass, took a brush through her red curls, and with a sigh watched them spring back into place. Considering it useless to fight her stubborn hair, she placed her brush on the dresser and grabbed her bag. She walked across the hall and stepped down the brown wooden staircase and past the family portraits and colorful tapestries from her parents' travels in Europe.

"Oh, Abigail, I'm so glad to see you. Are you feeling better?"

"I'm fine, Mother. I would like to go see Sophia, if you don't mind."

"Well, of course, dear. I'm afraid you'll have to drive yourself in the carriage. Your father is having a guest for dinner, and I have things to do. Can you manage?"

Abigail nodded. "Who's the guest?"

Her mother shook her head. "I don't know. Your father said he was going to town to employ a chauffeur and would invite him to dinner tonight."

Abigail smiled. "He will probably do it, too."

Her mother laughed, then said, "Oh, I do hope we find a chauffeur soon. I suppose we should have known Mr. Wickers would leave a great hole when he left."

"I miss him."

"I know you do, dear."

"Well, I'd better go hitch up the horses. I'll see you in a while." Abigail reached over and dropped a kiss on her mother's cheek.

Mother stretched her arms around her daughter. "I know you're in pain now," she whispered, "but it will fade with time. I promise." With a light pat on Abigail's back, her mother pulled away.

Abigail nodded, not wanting to think about it for fear she would cry again.

"Are you sure you don't want to eat first? You hardly touched your breakfast, Abigail." Mother's brows pushed together, scrunching a worry line between them.

Abigail touched her mother's arm. "I'm fine, really. I just wanted to talk a little with Sophia."

Though a worrisome frown still etched her face, her mother gave up with a sigh. "All right, you go and have a nice time. Give Sophia and her family our love. Oh, one more thing, Abigail."

Abigail turned back.

"If you happen by the mercantile, could you stop and pick up some coffee?"

Abigail smiled, nodded, and slipped through the door. With some effort, she hitched the horses to the carriage. Both horses.

Funny how things worked better in twos.

She did miss Mr. Wickers, but not only because he took them where they needed to go. He had been with the family for ten years and was practically like a grandpa to Abigail. Family had called him out west. Abigail wondered why people didn't stay in one place.

With a click of her tongue, she set the horses in motion. The Thread Bearer was situated a ways north of her home, so Abigail settled in and tried to relax for the ride.

Summer's sun had yet to give way to the call of autumn, though the intensity of its warmth had subsided somewhat. Green leaves waved from assorted trees located in a small city park. Abigail felt the need to turn in and meander through the winding lane. With a slight tug, she steered the horses through a path bordered with thick foliage and the season's last burst of blooms sprouting from plentiful plants.

The heady scent of roses followed her. She took a deep breath of the fresh, sweet air and allowed the peaceful surroundings to envelop her. Mothers sat along the few wooden benches, watching their children run and play in the expansive grasses. Abigail's eyes blurred. Would she ever know motherhood? She shook her head. Spurned by love once could happen to anyone. Only a fool would let it happen twice.

Her back straightened. She'd learned her lesson well. No need to go through it again. From this day forward, she would be on her guard. No other man would come close to her heart again. She'd see to that.

As she made her way through the edge of town, Abigail still marveled that last year's fire had left such devastation. People had rallied from all over the United States to lend a helping hand to Chicago. The railroad spilled immigrants into the city on a daily basis: people needing work, knowing

Chicago was rebuilding. "The land of opportunity." *Too bad Jonathan didn't feel that way.*

Though it would take time to rebuild, being the hub of importing and exporting goods, Chicago would survive. Already new structures stood taller and boasted brick faces, evidence of stricter building codes. Property values soared. The city throbbed with the excitement of new adventure.

Abigail figured if Chicago could move on after such devastation, so could she. Maybe she would put her teaching certificate to use and go to work somewhere. One thing she knew: She needed to leave her problems with her Savior. Only He had the answers, anyway.

Lord, please, grant me direction. Show me what Thy will is for me.

The horses snorted and neighed. Their harnesses jangled slightly as they plodded along the streets of Chicago. Though she loved the thrill of big city life, Abigail couldn't deny her longing for the quiet nights on the front porch of their family home, where crickets called from manicured bushes and fireflies flickered about on distant grassy meadows.

Seeing Manford's Mercantile, Abigail decided to stop and pick up coffee for her mother. Tying the horses to a hitching post, she made her way into the mercantile. Coffee and leather scents reached her the moment she entered. As she meandered through the aisles, the aroma of apples lifted from a nearby bin. Her footsteps left the scent behind and soon carried her to the sharp smell of pickles hovering around a barrel. She spotted the coffee and picked up a bag.

A slight temptation to dig into the jar of penny candy on the counter tickled her fancy, but with reluctance, she turned from it.

The thought of candy so engrossed her, she neglected to see the person in front of her until it was too late. She plowed into the man like a runaway horse cart slamming into a tree. He stopped cold.

A gasp caught in her chest. She looked up and peered into

dark brown eyes with golden flecks that seemed to fan from the center like sunlight bursting upon a brand-new day. The pleasure she saw in them warmed her down to her toes. "I–I'm so sorry. I don't know what must have gotten into me." She pulled out her handkerchief to cover her embarrassment, then stopped the dainty cloth at her throat as she attempted, but failed, to swallow.

A twinkle lit the man's dark eyes, making her almost light-headed. It was all she could do to hold herself up in her boots. Whatever had gotten into her, she didn't know, but one thing was for sure: She had to get over it.

"Ma'am, the fault was mine." In a polite gesture, he pulled off his hat, and a thatch of heavy blond hair spilled across his forehead. Her cheeks grew warm, and she knew her face must match her red hair. She had to get out of there before her heart jumped clean out of her chest. "If you'll excuse me," she said, pushing past him before he had a chance to say anything else. She started to leave the store when Mr. Manford called to her.

"Abigail?"

She turned and swallowed hard. "Yes?"

"You gonna pay for that coffee?"

She looked down at the package of coffee clutched to her chest. Her jaw dropped in astonishment. "Oh my!" she said, looking at Mr. Manford. Then without thought, she glanced toward the young man with the dark eyes. A full smile spread across his angular face. Could she possibly suffer any more humiliation? "I'm so sorry, Mr. Manford," she said in a whisper. He tried to hide his smile, but she saw it just the same. With shaky fingers, she pulled out her coin purse, plunked money on the counter, and scurried out the door.

❧

Titus Matthews's gaze met that of the storekeeper. Titus shook his head and smiled, then glanced back as the woman stepped out the door. Never before had he seen hair a blended color of autumn leaves. He picked up a sack of flour, but a vision of the woman's crimson face peered from the sack, her bright blue eyes coaxing him to find out her identity.

Maybe he could get her last name from the storekeeper. He'd have to be careful, though. Folks were suspicious of strangers. He shrugged. He might have to do his ma's shopping at Manford's Mercantile from now on in hopes of finding the woman again.

⌖

Once she arrived at the Thread Bearer, Abigail had settled down from her near bout with apoplexy at the mercantile. She climbed from the rig and tethered her horses. Lifting her heavy skirts, she stepped across muddy spots on the pathway and entered the shop. The bell jangled on the door behind her as she closed it.

"Be right with you," Sophia's voice called from the back room.

Abigail smiled and waited, knowing Sophia would be excited to see her. They hadn't visited in quite some time. Sophia had been too sick for church the last couple of weeks. Abigail needed to see how her friend was getting along.

Sophia stepped through the curtain that separated the rooms. "Abigail!"

The two women rushed through the room and embraced. "Oh, how I've missed you," Sophia said, quite out of breath. She pulled back and looked at her friend and gasped. "You've been crying. What's wrong?"

Abigail let out a chuckle and shook her head. "I could never get anything past you."

"Let me make some tea. Come to the back, won't you?"

"Am I keeping you from any deadlines?"

"No," Sophia called over her shoulder. "In fact, this is a very good day for a visit. I have only a few items to mend and one dress to start with no set date by which to deliver it."

Abigail pushed aside the curtain and sat at the scrubbed pine table while Sophia busied herself in the kitchen, putting water on the stove. Once the cups and saucers were placed on the table, Sophia sat down to wait for the heated water. "So, tell me what's going on." Her worried eyes met Abigail's.

Abigail sighed, not knowing exactly where to begin. "Well," she said, looking at her hands and fidgeting with her fingers, "Jonathan has moved back east."

"What?" Sophia's mouth gaped, her gaze fixed on Abigail. "Is someone in his family ill?"

Abigail shook her head. "It seems," she measured her words evenly, "he has a new position."

Sophia covered Abigail's hand with her own. "Oh, Abby, I'm so sorry."

Despite Abigail's great efforts, a tear trickled down her cheek and plopped onto the table. She quickly brushed it off with her hand.

"Oh, my dear, dear friend." Sophia stood, came around to the back of her chair, and gave her a hug.

Abigail rather wished Sophia hadn't been so compassionate. It made her want to crumple into a mass of tears.

The water on the stove boiled. Sophia stepped over and lifted the pan holding the hot liquid, pouring it into a teapot to steep their tea. "I can't believe you haven't told me this before now, Abigail."

"Well, you've been away from church, and to tell you the truth, I had no idea of his intentions until a week ago. I felt sure he would change his mind. I couldn't imagine he was serious. But I was wrong. He came by this morning, wished me well, and walked out of my life."

Sophia seemed to sense Abigail's need to stay composed. They waited a little while in silence. Sophia finally got up and walked over to the teapot. Pouring the steaming tea into their cups, Sophia placed Abigail's in front of her.

"Thank you."

Once seated, Sophia took a sip of her own drink.

Abigail gingerly swallowed the hot brew, willing it to calm her queasiness.

Placing her cup back in the saucer, Sophia looked Abigail

square in the face. "Well, that's that," she said matter-of-factly. "God has something better in store for you."

Abigail raised her hand to stop the conversation. "No no no!"

Sophia looked at her, puzzled. "What do you mean?"

"He might have something better in store for me, but I can tell you it doesn't include a man. Those days are over for me."

Sophia gasped. "Abigail, you can't mean that. You're too young. You have your whole life ahead of you."

"I assure you, Sophia, I do mean that."

Sophia seemed to stop herself from saying any more. "Well, I won't attempt to haggle with your Irish temper, but I will pray for you," she said with an ornery grin.

Abigail returned a weak smile.

Sophia leaned over and touched Abigail's arm. "Just promise me this. You'll be open to whatever the Lord has for you?"

Abigail nodded. "As long as my heart is not at risk." Even as she said the words, the image of the young man at the mercantile popped into her mind.

She wondered why.

two

Titus Matthews ran his hand through his hair, waited a moment, then pulled the watch from his pocket. Four o'clock. He had been walking the streets of Chicago since eight thirty in the morning and still no sign of a job. He looked around for a bench to rest his aching feet. Not seeing any, he moved on.

There had been plenty of ads listed in the *Chicago Tribune*, but it seemed someone always beat him to it. He thought they always needed railroad men, but with the great number of new workers coming into town, the competition grew fierce. His boot shoved a pebble out of the way. Why had his pa agreed to that investment? Why had he placed so much of the family earnings in one pot?

Titus's brown boots thumped hard against the dirt path, anger kicking up dust behind him. "Thomas O'Connor, you will pay for what you did to my pa and to our family," he groused, making his way across the road.

He decided to make one more stop at the mercantile. Though he had checked it out earlier, this time he decided he'd go back and pick up some things he remembered his ma needed. He doubted he'd run into the woman again, but then anything was possible. Not that it mattered. What woman wanted a man without a job? He couldn't provide for his ma and sister, let alone court a lady friend.

He entered Manford's Mercantile. He'd heard his ma say she had a craving for an apple pie. Ma loved to bake. Yet since Pa died, she had had few supplies with which to work. No more familiar smells of boiled chicken and beef or home-baked pies. His teeth clenched, jaw tightened. Resentment churned in his stomach.

Today, he aimed to change that.

She needed three apples and some sugar. Though funds were low, Titus decided he would get those for her. She had endured enough in the last six months, losing her husband and caring for a ten-year-old daughter who couldn't walk and hadn't said a word since Pa died in March. Though Titus's ma helped with some sewing, she brought in little income. The responsibility weighed heavily upon his shoulders.

"Good afternoon, Mr. Matthews," a strong voice called behind him.

Titus turned to look into the face of his enemy. Thomas O'Connor.

"Mr. O'Connor," he quipped and started to turn away.

"Wait," Thomas O'Connor said, placing a hand on Titus's arm.

Titus turned around.

"I don't know if you have a position just now, Titus, but I'm in desperate need of a chauffeur and wondered if—well, I wanted to know if you might help our family. I will pay you well," he quickly added.

Help their family, Titus sneered inside. Why, he'd rather spit at this man as to help his family. He took one step to walk away, when a thought struck him. Maybe he could help their family. More importantly, he could help his own family. This was his chance to get even with the man who took Pa's life, destroyed Titus's dreams of becoming a doctor, and took away the Matthewses' fine family home, leaving them to live in poverty in a hovel. Sure, he would help him—and make some money at the same time.

"Titus?"

Titus shook himself from his web of thoughts. "I would be much obliged, sir," he managed.

"Great!" Thomas O'Connor said, slapping Titus on the back. "Here's my address." He handed Titus a piece of paper. "Come by this evening for dinner, say, around seven o'clock, and we'll discuss your duties."

"I'll be there," Titus said, stuffing the address into his pocket.

The two men parted, and Titus felt good about getting the sugar and apples. Still, he couldn't deny a gnawing feeling in his gut, something that told him he'd better beware, that he might be stepping on shaky ground. He pushed the thought aside, allowing the bitterness to prevail. Besides, he had a right to feel the way he did.

Didn't he?

❧

Abigail looked up from the newspaper when her father came in the front door. "Hello, Father." She glanced at his parcel. "Oh dear, did you bring mother some coffee, too?"

He looked at his bag, then back at Abigail. "Don't tell me you stopped at the mercantile today?"

She laughed and nodded.

He chuckled. "Well, looks like we won't be running out of coffee for some time."

With a long apron draped over her ample middle, Abigail's mother came into the drawing room, stepping lightly on the plush rug at her feet. "What's this? Both of you stopped for coffee?" She placed her hands firmly on her hips and looked at them, a smudge of flour on the tip of her nose.

At the sight of her mother, Abigail smiled. She knew her father had tried time and again to talk Mother into hiring a cook, but she wouldn't hear of it. Her one joy in life, she always said, was to feed her family well.

"Yes, dear," Father said, dabbing at the flour on her nose, then bending to kiss her.

Mother laughed and took the sack from him. "Well, I suppose it will keep."

"So, what are we having for dinner?" Father followed her into the kitchen. Abigail wanted to hear about the surprise guest, so she trailed behind.

"We're having fried chicken, mashed potatoes, sliced carrots, and applesauce. Apple pie for dessert with coffee." Abigail couldn't help noticing Mother's pleasure.

"I'm sorry I wasn't home to help you cook today, Mother."

"Nonsense." She waved her hand. "I had a delightful day in the kitchen."

Abigail smiled, knowing how her mother loved to cook. She turned to her father. "Who's coming for dinner?" Abigail didn't miss the shadow that flickered across his face.

"Titus Matthews."

Mother turned to him. "Abram's boy?"

Father nodded. "Only he's not a boy, Lavina. He's a man. I'd say about Abby's age."

Abigail had no idea what any of it meant. "Who is Abram?"

Father pulled in a deep breath and pushed it out with effort. "He was a friend whom I tried to help. His business dealings were failing. I talked him into starting an insurance company. I partnered with him, and we insured many of the businesses that thrived before the fire."

Understanding hit Abigail. "You mean—"

Father nodded. "We lost it all. Couldn't pay the claims. Too many. It didn't really affect our family. I have our money divested in many different areas. Abram kept buying up more stock. I didn't want to pry into his affairs. I figured he had gotten back on his feet with his other investments. He wanted full ownership. I sold all my shares over to him a week before the fire. I only started the business to help him in the first place. What I didn't know until recently was that he had put everything in that business. When he died in March, he left his family with nothing but debt."

"Oh, how awful," Abigail said.

Mother went over and touched his arm. "You can't blame yourself, Thomas. Abram chose to do those things."

Father ran a hand through his thinning hair. "I know. I still can't get it out of my mind, though."

"So why are you having Titus over?" Mother asked, poking a fork into the potatoes on the stove.

He smiled. "I've asked him to be our new chauffeur."

She dropped the fork on the stove and turned to look at him with wide eyes. "And he agreed?"

Sadness touched Father's face once again. "He lost his job last week. Needs work." He rubbed his chin a moment. "Course I'll pay him more than the job is worth."

"Thomas, it's fine to do that if you want to help him, but don't do it because you feel guilty."

"I can't help but think I'd want someone to help you and Abby if I were gone."

Mother reached up and kissed him on the cheek.

"Abigail, you might want to help us out in the conversation. I'm a little on the slow side of things with young folks."

Abigail nodded out of respect. The last thing she wanted to do was spend her evening entertaining a gentleman.

"Is he married, have a family, Thomas?" Mother wanted to know.

"No. The way I understand it, he lives with his ma and sister. His sister, Jenny, fell from a horse a few years back, leaving her crippled. Titus was going to medical school, studying to be a doctor, until Abram died and the boy had to drop out."

Mother looked at Abigail. A cold knot formed in the pit of Abigail's stomach. She hoped her mother's cooking plans were for dinner only, not romance.

"When will he be here?" Mother asked.

Father had grabbed the paper and was already on the finance page. "Hmm?"

"Thomas, when will Mr. Matthews be here?" she asked again with a nip of impatience.

He glanced up. "Oh, sorry, dear. Should be here. . ." He glanced at his pocket watch. "Any minute now." He looked up and smiled.

"Oh, you," she said, flicking the towel at him before she commenced to flutter about the kitchen in a flurry, handing out orders to Abigail. "Abby, get the dishes so we can set the table. Oh dear, where are our good bowls?" Mother asked no one in particular as she fished through the cupboards.

Her ramblings were cut short when a knock sounded at the front door.

"That would be our guest," Father said with a smile. He folded the newspaper back in place and headed to the door.

"Oh, just a minute," Abigail said, racing past him to run up the stairs to her room. Once she reached the top of the stairway, she turned to look at her father, who watched her with his hand on the doorknob. "All right, now you can let him in."

He laughed and shook his head. Abigail saw him twist the door handle. She darted out of sight and into her room. Not that she cared one way or another what some man thought about her. Still, she didn't want to look like an old hag.

Quickly, she slipped from her soiled clothing and put on a fresh combination of a sensible white top and black skirt. As usual, her curls bounced in unruly ringlets. She pulled the abundance of hair into a shapely knot at the back of her neck. A few ringlets slipped from the pins and sprung loosely at the sides of her face. She sighed. "It's hopeless," she said to her reflection. Taking a deep breath, she left her room and headed down the stairs.

She could hear her parents talking to Titus. His voice was deep, confident. Reminded her of someone else. Jonathan. No, she wouldn't think about that tonight. She would make the chauffeur feel welcome, make polite conversation, and go to bed. She was having a miserable day, and the sooner it was over, the better.

He most likely would consider her an old maid. A spinster. How embarrassing—although not as embarrassing as her earlier escapade at the mercantile. At the time, she had been mortified, though right now, as the whole scene played out in her mind, she thought it quite funny. She felt a smile light her face just as she walked into the kitchen.

"Ah, Abigail, dear. I'd like you to meet our new chauffeur, Titus Matthews."

The young man turned from Father and looked at her. Abigail nearly swallowed her tongue. The same dark eyes that had earlier made her almost trip on her boots looked back at her.

At first, surprise etched his features, then something else. What it was, Abigail couldn't be sure. "Well, hello again," he said.

"Um, he—hello."

"You two have met?" Father asked with a puzzled grin.

Titus turned to him. "Yes, in fact, only this afternoon. In the mercantile."

Father glanced from Titus to Abigail. "Ah, yes, the coffee." He threw a wink at his daughter. She wanted to throw a towel at him.

Oh, why did she have to stay and make conversation? She wanted to go to her room. This man made her uncomfortable, though she wasn't sure why. After all, it wasn't his fault his presence lifted her to a hazy vision of a crackling hearth on a winter's day. Goodness, how could those thoughts pop in her mind when she had said good-bye to the love of her life only that morning?

"Abigail?" Mother was saying.

"I'm sorry?"

Everyone looked at her.

"Would you help me carry the serving dishes to the table, please?"

"Oh, yes." Abigail quickly ran to help.

Once the table was laden with an abundance of food, the group settled themselves quite comfortably in the dining chairs, and Father led them in prayer. Titus cleared his throat and shifted in his seat. Abigail wondered of his thoughts toward God. Was he bitter because of his pa's death and the circumstances in which he now found himself? She'd have to remember to pray for him.

Amid the clinking of silverware against dinner plates, Abigail felt the conversation moved along at a reasonable pace. Before long, she felt herself actually relax and steal a glance or two at the gentleman seated across from her. So different in appearance from Jonathan, and yet something about him. . .

She snapped her cloth napkin back in place at her lap. No

matter how nice or friendly he seemed, she would keep her distance. Although she did not want to be un-Christian, she would not allow herself another heartache. The more she could avoid their new chauffeur, the better.

She took a bite of potatoes and glanced up in time to see Titus looking at her. He smiled. She turned away and struggled to swallow.

Yes, she would avoid him.

❧

"Titus, did you have a nice dinner?" his ma asked as he settled into the chair and pulled off his boots.

"Yeah, it was fine, Ma." He attempted to keep the agitation from his voice.

He looked up in time to see a frown on Ma's face. He let out a long breath. "Sorry, Ma. I'm just a little tired."

She gave a short nod. "Would you like some tea or coffee?" she asked in a whisper. His sister, Jenny, slept on a mat in the corner of the room.

"No, thanks. I'm going to bed, too." He rose to his feet, clutching his boots with his right hand.

"Titus."

He winced within. Nothing got past his ma. He looked to her.

"They're good people. Things happen beyond our control."

He shrugged as if he had no idea to what she was referring.

Her eyes sparked with understanding. "Bitterness never helped anybody."

"I don't know what you're talking about, Ma."

"Sit back down."

Reluctantly, he complied.

"I see the blame in your eyes, Titus. Your heart has grown cold. I know your dreams have been put on hold for now—"

"On hold? Is that what you think, Ma?" His hands slid down his stubbled jaw. "They're not on hold. They're gone," he said with finality.

"I don't believe that," she insisted. "The Lord gave you a

love for people and the intelligence to help them. He'll see that you use your gifts. Trust Him."

His jaw clenched. It wasn't Ma's fault things turned out this way. He wouldn't take it out on her.

"Don't allow bitterness to separate you from your Lord and your gifts. You'll have a much different future, Son, if you give in to this temptation."

"Meaning no disrespect, but I'm going to bed, Ma."

She lifted her chin. "Mind you, my prayers will not let you go. I can be as stubborn as you are." Her expression emphasized her words.

He lifted a slight smile, walked over to Ma, and kissed her on the forehead. As he started to walk away, she grabbed his arm. "I will bombard heaven 'til you set things right in your heart, Titus Matthews."

"You're right. You are stubborn." He winked at her and walked away.

Once ready to go to sleep, he settled onto his makeshift bed on the floor. The wooden boards that held their tiny home together creaked and groaned with the night winds, reminding him of the depths to which they had fallen. He pulled the thin blanket up around him to shut out the draft seeping through the boards. How could he not be bitter?

Thoughts of Abigail played upon his mind, adding to his bitterness. Why couldn't they have met under other circumstances, another time? He couldn't deny his attraction to her, but he wouldn't entertain that thought. She was an O'Connor. Plain and simple. And O'Connor was a name he planned to bring down. He didn't know how or when, but he figured every family had a weak spot, a place of secrets that the outside world didn't see. His job was to find their weakness and expose them to all of Chicago.

A cold chill whipped through him. He buried himself deeper into his blanket. Yes, he would bring the proud O'Connor family down.

Just like they had done to the Matthews family.

three

Abigail walked onto the porch and glanced up at the moisture-laden clouds. She went back inside and grabbed an umbrella from a tall basket, then stepped back outside. A carriage creaked and rattled as it rolled past her house. Neighbors Jack and Nan Forrest waved at Abigail. She returned the greeting. Just then her attention turned to the wheels of another carriage that bit into the hard ground and ultimately came to a halt in front of the porch.

Titus jumped from his seat and walked over to her. He took off his hat. "Miss O'Connor."

"Good afternoon," she said with a smile. "And please, call me Abigail."

His eyes twinkled with pleasure. "Abigail then." He stood a moment, as if forgetting the task at hand. "Where would you like to go?"

She smiled. "Have you heard of the work that goes on at Barnabas House, located in the Irish neighborhood?" She didn't miss the surprise on his face.

He nodded.

"I want to go there." She thought she noticed a look of disapproval flicker upon his face.

He hesitated. "That's no place for a lady, Abigail. Are you certain?"

Why, by giving her such advice, he had quickly taken on an air of familiarity that she wasn't at all sure she liked. In fact, she felt quite sure she didn't like it. Her back bristled. Her parents approved of the work at Barnabas House, and she certainly did not need the approval of the family chauffeur. "It is a respected program put on by one of the churches in town. I am certain," she said with finality.

His right eyebrow rose, his gaze never leaving her eyes. He looked almost as if he dared challenge her request. Why, of all the nerve. What was his problem? She lifted her gloved hand, letting him know the discussion had ended, and he could now help her onto the seat of the open carriage.

Which he did.

Once on the seat, she settled in for the ride, straightening her skirt, adjusting her hat, fingering her loose strands of hair back into place. Though it did little good. With the open carriage, her hat barely held her hair in place. She didn't know what to think of Titus's response. What was it to him where she went? He wasn't her husband, after all. She wasn't about to let the family chauffeur tell her what to do.

Her shoulders heaved as she sighed. Her Irish temper would get the better of her if she wasn't careful. It was the one temptation to which she succumbed almost daily. Abigail bit her lip. *Why can't I work past that, Lord? Sophia has the sweetest demeanor, calm, peaceful. I flit around my little world, barking at anything that stands in my way.*

She kept peering to the right of her, being careful not to look at Titus on her left. She gazed absently at the passing scenery. *My temper is my thorn in the flesh, I suppose,* she thought. With another sigh, she attempted to calm herself before arriving to work at Barnabas House.

The carriage continued, jostling about as it traveled over potholes and ridges in the dirty streets. The scenery had turned from sprawling houses with plush green lawns, pruned bushes, and rambling honeysuckle vines, to tattered yards splotched with mud holes, random sprouts of grass, tangled weeds, and overgrown bushes.

Trash littered the streets, and dirty children played in front of the tenements. Rats searched through discarded debris in hidden alleyways. Hundreds of houses were unconnected with the street sewer. Abigail's heart bled for her people. The Irish were her people, weren't they? She shrugged off the doubt. With her red hair and temper, she figured she had to be related.

God had been merciful to her, placing her at the O'Connors' front door when she was a mere three days old. Countless times, Mother had told her shortly after they found out they couldn't have children, Abigail had shown up in a basket on their porch. Nothing short of a miracle. Abigail smiled at God's kindness. . .to all of them.

She would live her life in thankfulness to Him by helping the Irish immigrants. Even if they weren't her blood relatives, the O'Connors were related, and well, she was an O'Connor.

That was enough for her.

❧

Titus pulled the carriage to a stop, and Abigail waited for him to help her down. Once they walked a few feet, the stench from the stables wafted over her, taking her breath away. She wanted to grab a handkerchief but didn't want to offend the people. She told herself she could do this.

Helping her over some mud holes, Titus saw her to the edge of the property.

"Thank you, Mr. Matthews."

"Please, it's Titus."

"Titus," she repeated. "I'll most likely be here an hour or so. You might check back around five o'clock?"

"I have nothing else to do. I'll wait here."

She had a sneaking suspicion he was playing the guardian again, but distracted by the poverty, she left his comment alone. "As you wish." She stepped past him and made her way through the door.

Dark with shadows, the room smelled of sweat and dirt. The outside stench seeped sparingly through the open cracks. Despair met her through the eyes of the people. Abigail mentally rolled up her sleeves. First thing on her agenda was to make the place look happy. The former drawing room needed paint. Lots of it.

"Abigail O'Connor?" a masculine voice called beside her. She turned to him.

The man had raven black hair and a charming smile, and

hidden only slightly behind wired spectacles were blue eyes that sparkled like Lake Michigan on a sunny day. She liked him instantly.

"Hello. I'm Christopher Doyle, director of Barnabas House."

"Hello, Mr. Doyle."

"Please, call me Christopher." Before she could comment, he continued. "Might I call you Abigail?"

She nodded.

"I'm afraid there's not much need for formalities here." His gaze swept around the room, causing Abigail to do the same. He turned back to her. "I understand you have a teaching certificate?"

"Yes."

"Good. Once the children return from school, we need someone to help them with their studies."

She nodded with understanding.

"Let's go over to the table where we can talk." He led the way. "Would you like some coffee?" he called over his shoulder.

"No, thank you."

They arrived at a wooden table marred and nicked with use. Christopher pulled out a seat for her. "We have five bedrooms upstairs where the cook, the cleaning lady and her child, and a couple of other workers stay. I have a room in the basement since I'm the only man." He smiled. "Neighbors come in for various supplies. Before handing out health items, we teach them about taking care of their bodies. With the distribution of free food, we discuss nutrition and proper eating. We cover the importance of being good neighbors and reaching out to those around us in need. They come to us to learn what job opportunities are available in the city, and we try to find the best jobs for them."

Abigail couldn't imagine such poverty with people struggling to afford the dilapidated dwellings she had witnessed in the neighborhood.

"I wish we could do more," Christopher said, looking absently ahead. He blew out a frustrated sigh and turned a weak smile her way. "The main thing is to get them off the streets, working, and into homes."

Abigail nodded.

"Well," he said, smacking the table with his hands, "that's where you come in." His broad smile was back. He then led Abigail to a group of five children, thin, wide-eyed, fair-skinned, with assorted freckles sprinkled across their noses. Her heart melted at the sight of them. Christopher introduced Abigail. They eagerly pulled out their school slates. The more talkative ones began chattering about their school assignments. Christopher smiled, then let her commence to work. She hardly noticed when he walked away. The children had already captured her attention. And her heart.

&

Titus grabbed a cup of coffee from a nearby store while he waited for Abigail. He passed some time talking with the neighborhood men, who groused about no work and poor living conditions. Titus barely tolerated the strong coffee but managed to get it down just the same. He had to agree the Irish neighborhood conditions were worse than what he and his family had to endure.

Of course, with people like Abigail O'Connor to help them. . .

He ignored the dip of his heart with the thought of her. His thoughts turned smug. *Abigail O'Connor and her charity work. Just like her father trying to salve his conscience by hiring me, most likely she, too, has something to hide.*

He would find out their weakness. It might take some time, but if he remained patient, they would crumble. He'd see to that.

After a while, he went back to the carriage and waited in his seat. The front doors finally creaked open, and his head jerked up.

"Thank you, again, Abigail, for your fine help today. I can see the children have immediately taken to you," the man beside her was saying. Abigail smiled at him and waved good-bye.

The sight of the man standing beside her brought an uncomfortable twist to Titus's gut. He jumped from his carriage seat and went over to escort her.

"Have you been waiting all this time?" Abigail asked.

"I went down the road and had some coffee, talked with a few of the neighbors."

Abigail looked at him for a moment. A pleasant smile came to her lips.

"What?"

"Oh, nothing," she said as he helped her onto the carriage. "We do have one more stop. I need to check on my gramma. She has been ill lately."

"All right. How do I get there?"

Abigail gave him directions, and soon they were on their way. Titus could see his days were going to be filled with carting Abigail around town. The horses *clip-clopped* their way through the dusty streets, and his mind wandered to the man at Barnabas House. He seemed a mite too friendly, to Titus's way of thinking. But then what was that to him? It's not like he cared one way or another how friendly the man was to Abigail. Two reformers. They deserved each other.

26.

Maeve O'Connor lifted hooded eyes to her granddaughter. "Good day to ye, Abigail darling," she said with a voice frail and thin as she settled into her deep chair.

Abigail slipped off her hat and crossed the floor to her gramma. Thin arms wound about Abigail's neck, and kisses pressed into the top of her burnished curls. The smell of medicines and sickness surrounded Abigail in the embrace. Once they parted, Abigail scooted a chair closer to the old woman.

"How are you feeling?"

"Ah," Gramma said with a wave of her hand, " 'tis better I'm getting. The doctor says this pneumonia won't kill me." She shrugged. " 'Tis me old, worn-out body takes a long time to mend, it does." A smile lit her lips and reflected in her eyes.

"I miss you, Gramma."

"And I be missing ye, too, Abigail darling." Then as if to dismiss sentimentality, Gramma picked up a lighthearted voice. "So, tell me now about ye chauffeur. I saw him when the carriage pulled up." She wiggled her eyebrows.

"Gramma, you've been spying!" Abigail said with a giggle.

Gramma shrugged with mischief. " 'Tis true," she admitted shamelessly. "And what else is it that an old woman is to do when she be bored?"

Abigail laughed again. "He is Titus Matthews."

"Quite the laddie," Gramma encouraged, all the while studying Abigail's face.

"Not a possibility," Abigail said, shaking her head. "I'm through with men." She used a carefree tone so as not to worry Gramma. She figured there was no need for anyone to know the depth of truth to her statement.

Gramma studied her a moment. "God has a plan, Abigail darling. Ye must trust Him." She pointed a bony finger toward her. A fit of coughing followed, causing Abigail to run for a glass of water. Once the coughing stopped, Abigail pushed the water to Gramma.

Abigail stayed close to her, dabbing at her face with a cool cloth. "Are you sure you're all right?"

Gramma raised a smile. "Ah, I be fine."

Abigail spent a pleasurable hour talking with Gramma and telling her about the work at Barnabas House.

As evening fell upon the city, Abigail kissed her gramma good-bye and walked toward the door.

"Abigail?" Gramma called.

She turned. "Yes?"

"I'll be asking ye the same question ye asked me, wee one. Are ye sure ye be all right?"

"I'm fine, Gramma. I'm fine." With that, Abigail turned and walked through the door. Her eyes locked with Titus's, and she prayed it was so.

four

By the time the carriage rolled to a stop, Abigail felt thankful to be home. She yawned just before climbing down, the lantern on the carriage lighting the way. A soft yellow light spilled from the house onto the outside lawn, giving Abigail some ability to see where she stepped. A small wail sounded behind the bushes.

"What's that?" Abigail stopped in her tracks, her finger pressed against her lips. Titus listened. Another cry. Together they edged forward, careful not to get too close to the bush. "I think something is back there and it's hurt," she whispered. With caution, she pulled apart a cluster of the bush and peered in. There sat a mutt covered in long, white hair with patches of brown thrown in seemingly as an afterthought. A blob of disheveled fur lopped over one eye, while his tongue drooped rather disgracefully from his mouth. Abigail glanced at his front paw. The bone poked in an odd angle.

"Oh, Titus, he's hurt."

"Watch it, Abigail. A dog in pain could bite."

She pulled back. "Will you get Father? We need to take him to the veterinarian."

Titus nodded and went to the house while Abigail cooed softly to the animal, trying to ease his pain.

In no time, the lucky hound went from rags to riches as the O'Connors swept him into the veterinarian's office, had his broken leg set, then whisked him happily off to his new home.

"Abigail, I have no idea what we're going to do with a dog," Mother said, staring with disapproval at the animal in the house. The dog seemed to sense her dislike. He hobbled over behind Abigail's legs.

Abigail chuckled. "Oh, you poor thing." She patted his head, then looked up at Mother. "I told you. I'll take care of him. You won't have to do a thing. I'm not a little girl anymore. I can handle it." Abigail scrunched down and scratched him behind his ears. "Besides, I think he will be a great encouragement to the children at Barnabas House."

With arms crossed, Mother looked him over once more and finally sighed. "Well, just see that you do care for him. I'll not have a dog tearing up our things around the house."

Feeling much like a child again, Abigail jumped up and gave Mother a squeeze. "Thank you."

Mother returned the embrace, then looked back at the dog. A sudden softness came to her voice. "The poor thing has been through enough for one day." She paused a moment before adding an admonishment. "But mind you, tomorrow he will have a bath. You'll just have to be careful of his leg."

Abigail nodded, then picked the dog up and carried him to her room, while Mother just shook her head and watched.

With her feet, Abigail maneuvered a small rug beside her bed. Carefully, she bent down and laid the dog on the rug. He looked up at her with dark, melting eyes. Abigail stroked his fur and talked in whispers, lulling the animal to sleep. She'd have to think of a name for him.

Quietly, she pulled off her clothes and changed into her nightgown. Sinking into her soft bed covers, she reached for her Bible and read a passage. Afterward, she placed it back on her stand, then glanced once more at the sleeping hound. "Barnabas. I think I'll call you Barnabas," she whispered. Satisfied, she blew a puff of air into the lamplight, snuffing the room into darkness.

Abigail rolled over to her side, pulling the covers just under her chin. It had been a long day but a rewarding one. Not until that very moment did she realize she hadn't thought about Jonathan the entire day.

Still, she wondered if he slept peacefully tonight in the comfort of his bedroom so very far away.

❧

The smell of breakfast alerted his nose, and Titus opened his eyes. Sausage? Eggs? He couldn't remember such a breakfast in some time. He sat up and stretched on his bed. He turned to the sounds of clanging pots and sizzling bacon.

"Well, good morning, sleepyhead," his ma said with a smile. She finished setting the table. Thrusting himself from his bed, he stretched his tired muscles and walked over to the table. Jenny sat smiling from her chair. Ma had pulled Jenny's blond hair back from her face into a long braid. Hollow eyes looked up at him. Titus's heart flipped with the sight of his little sister. So weak. So vulnerable. He grinned back at her. "Boy, I love Sundays! The one day I can be home. Right, Jenny girl?" He reached over and ruffled the hair on top of her head, then turned to Ma. "How long 'til breakfast is ready?"

"Almost ready," Ma said, turning the eggs in the pan.

"If you don't mind, I'll step outside for a breath of air so it can wake me up. I'll be right back."

She nodded as she placed steaming biscuits on the table.

Walking into the backyard, Titus felt the morning chill prick his skin as he surveyed the area. Weather-beaten homes with sagging porches stumbled over one another along the street, leaving no gaps between neighbors. Broken glass, tattered furniture, and fragments of yesterday's trinkets littered neglected lawns. Being one for privacy, Titus hated the intrusion of other people so close to his home. He could hear their conversations, their *thumps* across wooden floors, their heated arguments. He shook his head. It wasn't like him to dwell in resentment, but he was there for now and wasn't ready to give it up. Not until somebody paid.

By the time he stepped into the kitchen, Ma was seated beside Jenny, and they both looked up at him. "Oh, sorry, didn't mean to take so long." He quickly seated himself and reached for a biscuit. Ma's words stopped him.

"Dear Lord, we thank Thee for the wonderful meal this morning. We ask that Thou wouldst bless the kind people who so graciously shared of their abundance with us. In Jesus' name, amen."

Titus knew their family tradition of prayer before meals, but he found himself forgetting such things more and more each day. He reached for a biscuit and pulled it open. Careful to save some for Ma and Jenny, he spread a tiny dollop of butter inside. "So, which *kind* person shared with us today?" Titus bit into his biscuit and looked at Ma.

She didn't even blink at his snide remark. "The Barnabas House brought some food over for us yesterday," she said matter-of-factly, while spooning some food onto her plate.

The impact of her statement hit him full in the face. He stopped chewing and glared at her. "Abigail O'Connor," he said with distaste.

Ma looked up pleasantly. "I would suspect so. Very kind of her and—"

He hit the table with his fist, stopping her words. His lips snarled, and he shoved his plate away. "How ironic that they would help us!" He barely spat out the words. "We don't need *their* charity! The O'Connor family brought this on us in the first place!"

Ma's face turned red. "Now, you listen here, young man. You'll be going to an early grave, talking like that. The O'Connors are good people. Your pa made a choice. It turned out to be bad. Nobody is to blame. Things happen. The good Lord—"

"I don't want to hear about the good Lord," he shouted, rising to his feet.

Ma rose to her feet, too. "You'll not be talking like that in this house, Titus Matthews!" A whimper sounded from the table, causing them to turn to Jenny. Tears streamed steadily down her face.

As angry as he was, Titus couldn't hurt his sister. He swallowed hard and took a deep breath as the anger slinked away. Ma and Titus exchanged a glance. Titus walked over to Jenny and hugged her. "It's all right, Jenny." He held her tight, kissing the top of her head. "I'm sorry. I was wrong." He felt tears moisten his eyes. How could he do this to Jenny when she had so much to deal with already? "Ma. . .is right," he heard himself saying, though he refused to believe it.

Jenny hiccuped a time or two, then wiped her tears. Ma settled back in her place, and Titus did the same. They finished their meal in silence.

After breakfast, Ma cleared the table and grabbed her Bible. With Jenny's inability to walk, they found it too difficult to get to church, so Ma saw to it that they got religious training through her daily reading of the scriptures.

Out of respect, Titus stayed in his seat, but it took everything in him to keep himself there. After years of hearing the scriptures, he could recite verses without thinking. But they rang hollow in his dark heart. He knew he was traveling a path better left alone, but he couldn't seem to stop himself. Bitterness fed on his soul like termites on wood.

Hadn't King David of the scriptures avenged himself on his enemies? Titus tried to convince himself of that, but he knew his thoughts were a distortion of the truth. David had left Saul alone, though countless times Saul had tried to kill David. David left his enemies in God's hands.

Enough! Ma had filled his mind over the years with Bible teachings, making him weak. He needed to think like a man, not a weakling who depended on God as a crutch. No, this was one battle he could handle himself.

❧

Abigail walked across the lawn to the stables in search of Titus, the morning dew soaking the hem of her dress. She peered into the barn. "Titus?"

At her side, merely a breath away, he answered. "Yes?"

She turned to face him. His breath was close enough to cause her face to tingle. "Oh," she said with a gasp. She took an awkward step back, tripping over her skirts. He reached out his hand and grabbed her to keep her from falling backward. For a moment, he hovered over her slightly bent form and looked down into her eyes. Neither said a word. A horse neighed, seeming to bring Titus to his senses. He looked as though he'd been splashed with cold water. Pulling Abigail to a standing position, he cleared his throat. "Are you all right?"

Abigail's hand pressed hard against her chest. "I'm fine. I don't know what got into me." She looked around a moment, not knowing how to handle the situation. Finally, she lifted her head and looked back at him. "I wanted to let you know I won't be going anywhere until this afternoon when it's time to go to Barnabas House. So if you want to groom the horses, you'll have the time." She pulled at her handkerchief and gave a delicate cough.

"Thank you. I'll do that."

She nodded, then turned to go.

"Did you have Barnabas House bring our family food on Saturday?"

She stopped in place. Did she hear resentment in his voice? Maybe she had stepped out of line. Father had said the Matthews family was proud. She turned to him. "Well, I might have mentioned your ma could be in need of a few items."

Looking a bit uncomfortable, he hesitated a moment. He rolled his hat around in his hands a few seconds before looking back at her. "Thanks."

Relief washed over her. "You're welcome." She felt herself smile.

In fact, she smiled all the way back to the house.

❧

Titus brushed the horses with more vigor than necessary. Had he really thanked her for her charity? What had gotten into him? He knew the answer all too well.

Those blue eyes. The way her curls spilled across her shoulders and reflected the brilliance of the morning sun. Her kindness and gentle ways.

He yanked off his hat and slapped it against his pant leg. "It's not supposed to be like this!" he grumbled to the horses. "I have my plan all set, and I don't need Abigail O'Connor to mess things up." He plunked his hat back on and brushed the horse's coat once again. If his plans were to succeed, he'd have to stay away from Abigail, keep his relationship with her strictly business. He could do this.

He had to.

⁊

"Abigail, are you all right?" Mother asked when Abigail stepped into the house, quite out of breath.

She looked up with a start. "Oh, yes, I'm fine."

"Look at the hem of your skirt," Mother said, pointing. "Where have you been?"

"Oh, I went out to tell Titus I wouldn't be going anywhere until this afternoon if he wanted to groom the horses."

Her mother studied her a moment.

"What?" Abigail asked, feeling uncomfortable under her mother's scrutiny.

"Oh, nothing," Mother said with a smile. "Nothing at all."

Abigail wasn't sure what that meant, but she knew one thing. She didn't like the sounds of it. Not one bit.

Making her way up the stairs, Abigail went to her bedroom. She needed to take Barnabas outside. When she pushed through the door, she saw the dog standing, admittedly a little crooked, waiting on her. Abigail laughed and walked over to him.

His tail wagged furiously as she edged closer; thankful eyes looked to her. Abigail bent down to the animal, speaking words of comfort to him. She wanted to nuzzle him but decided since she hadn't given him a bath yet, she'd better wait. Instead, she scratched the top of his head and worked her fingers down his back. He leaned in toward her as if begging for more. Father had found an old leash and collar in the barn and brought them in the night before. Abigail fastened the collar around Barnabas's neck, then clamped on the leash. She carried him down the stairs, but once they reached the bottom, she lowered him to the floor, allowing him to adjust to his new way of walking.

"I'm taking Barnabas outside, Mother," she called before opening the door. Once outside, Abigail took Barnabas to a secluded spot in the backyard. She lifted her face to the morning sun, allowing its warm rays to wash over her. The warmth gave her a good feeling. Like when she and Jonathan shared happy times together. Jonathan. Her good feeling plunged. She lowered her head. "Where are you, Jonathan? Do you miss me at all?"

Just then, Barnabas stood erect. His body tensed, muscles flexed. A low, menacing growl simmered in his throat, and his lips rolled back, revealing pointed teeth.

Abigail turned. "Titus. You startled me."

"Oh, I'm sorry," he said. "Looks like you've got a good watchdog, though."

Abigail laughed. "I guess I do," she said, rewarding Barnabas with a scratch on the head.

"I saw you out here and thought I'd find out what time you were thinking of leaving this afternoon. I wanted to clean out the stalls."

"Oh, probably around three o'clock. Will that work for you?"

"That's fine." He stood there for a moment. "Well, that's all I needed."

She nodded and smiled. Abigail watched as he walked away. Funny he should come out here to ask her that. She thought he had known they would leave at three. Could it be he was looking for an excuse to talk to her? She couldn't help feeling a little giddy at the thought. But then, what woman didn't appreciate a little attention from a handsome gentleman once in a while?

You're through with men, remember? The thought rang in her ears. *Of course, I remember.* "Come on, Barnabas, time to go in." The dog instantly hobbled to her side. She could hardly wait until three o'clock. The children would enjoy meeting Barnabas.

Or was she looking forward to three o'clock for another reason?

five

The autumn winds swept the rest of September and all of October right into history. Abigail pulled her dark, woolen cloak tight against her as she stepped into the wintry November chill. Titus tipped his hat. "Abigail." She smiled and offered Barnabas to him as she stepped up to her carriage seat. Once she situated herself, Titus gave the hound a friendly scratch and lifted Barnabas to her. The two laughed as they watched the dog curl up in her lap.

Titus climbed onto the carriage and flicked the horses into a steady trot. "Barnabas seems to be getting around a lot better since his leg has healed."

She nodded.

"His fur looks better, too, since he's moved in with your family. You're taking mighty fine care of him." Titus reached over and stroked the dog down his back, causing Barnabas's left hind leg to stretch with delight.

Titus and Abigail laughed. "Looks like you've won him over at last," she said with a smile.

"I don't know who's won who over," Titus admitted. "But one thing's for sure: Those kids at the house love him."

Abigail warmed to his words. "Yes, they do." She gave Barnabas an affectionate hug. Then remembering something, she turned to Titus. "Oh, don't let me forget. Ma said we need to stop at the post office and check the mail."

He nodded.

The afternoon went by quickly as Abigail worked with the children. Their studies seemed to be going well, and she enjoyed each of them. Abigail gathered her things to prepare to leave. She turned to see Katie O'Grady hugging Barnabas tight against her. In characteristic charm, a thatch of white hair drooped over the dog's right eye. His gentle face seemed to hold a smile, suggesting he was quite fond of the children's hugs. He snuggled his face into the crook of Katie's arm, as if totally enjoying the warmth of her embrace.

Abigail softened at the sight. Her heart went out to Katie. Only six years old, the child had suffered much already. Her pa left their family shortly after they arrived in America, just a few years back. Struggling to make ends meet, Katie's ma cleaned Barnabas House in return for room and board for herself and her daughter.

Abigail wondered how Mary O'Grady got through each day knowing the man she had given her life to had walked out on her and their child. Sadly, he could never come back. Shortly after leaving his family, he had stepped off a curb in the dark of night and been hit by a carriage. He died the next day. Such a tragedy. That's what Abigail couldn't risk. A man promising to love her forever, then leaving. Like Jonathan.

"I love Barnabas," Katie said when she saw Abigail watching them.

"I know you do." Abigail cringed, thinking that a man could abandon his family in this way. But then isn't that what happened to her? Her parents had left her on the doorstep of the O'Connor family. Did her real parents know the O'Connors? Somehow, Abigail felt her parents did know them and knew that they would take good care of her. And the O'Connors had been wonderful parents. Still, sometimes she craved to know where she belonged. Where were her roots? Were her parents still living?

Abigail felt a tug on her leg and looked down. "Yes, Katie?"

The little girl clung to Abigail's dress and through messy hair looked up. "I love you, Miss Abigail." She squeezed Abigail's skirts once more.

Without warning, tears sprang to Abigail's eyes. She related to this child in many ways. After all, she, too, had been abandoned. By her parents. By Jonathan. Abigail hunkered down to the child. "And I love you, Katie O'Grady," she said, hugging the child with abandon.

"You won't ever leave me, will you, Miss Abigail?"

Abigail's breath caught in her throat. Only God knew the future. How could she make a promise she wasn't sure she could keep?

"I will be here, Katie, for as long as I'm able."

The child seemed satisfied with the answer and squeezed her once more before trotting off to play with the rag doll Abigail had given her weeks ago.

"Come, Barnabas," Abigail called. Once the hound was on a leash, she waved good-bye to the children and made her way out to the carriage. The strain of the child's sincere question had tired Abigail. She kept her tears at bay, refusing to think further on parents who abandoned children and gentlemen who left broken hearts behind.

❧

Titus pulled the carriage to a stop in front of the post office. Abigail waited as he opened the door for her. "I'll only be a moment," she said, making her way to the door.

Once inside, she exchanged pleasantries with the woman who ran the post office. The woman then pulled Abigail's mail from the proper box and handed it to her. Abigail sorted through it and looked curiously upon one parcel in particular. A letter from Uncle Edward out in Colorado Territory. Why would he be writing to their family? She fingered the envelope, turning it over in her hands. Uncle Edward had cheated her father out of a job at least fifteen years ago. Pa forgave him, even tried to keep in touch, but Uncle Edward avoided his brother. Father had said Edward needed the Lord and they should pray for him, Aunt Elizabeth, and their daughter, Eliza. Her father had prayed faithfully over the years. The letter could bring good news. The mere fact he was writing would encourage Father, she felt sure.

Abigail thought of her cousin. Eliza and her pa were just alike in looks. . .and behavior. Spoiled, mean, and selfish.

Remembering her mother's scolding on the subject over the

years, Abigail chided herself for such thoughts. After all, those were childish pranks Eliza had pulled, tattling and lying to the adults. They were grown up now. Abigail wondered what had happened to Eliza.

She could hardly wait to get home and get the mail to her parents.

"Good news?" Titus asked, helping her back into the carriage.

"Possibly," she said, holding up the letter.

"I'm glad," Titus answered. A look of affection flittered across his face. Abigail was pleased she had noticed.

❧

Abigail and Mother sat on the sofa in the drawing room while Father opened the letter. The solemn look on his face made Abigail a little uneasy. Concern shadowed Mother's face, as well.

"Thomas, what is it?" Mother asked.

He rubbed his chin and thought for a moment, as if searching for the right words. "Well, it seems Edward has been down on his luck. The gold rush didn't work out. He's in Colorado Territory now and without work."

Ma lifted her chin.

He held out his palm. "Now, hold on, Lavina. Before you get yourself out of sorts, let me finish." He dropped his hand and glanced at the letter again. "It seems they barely have food on the table. Eliza is down to skin and bones, and he fears for her. He says here that since we're good Christian folks—" Father glanced up. "He's sending Eliza to live with us."

Ma gasped. "What?"

Abigail felt her stomach turn to lead. All the childhood memories once again burned across her mind like a fire out of control. How silly, she thought, pushing the immature matter aside. She looked at Mother, who seemed to bite her tongue. "What is it?" Abigail asked.

No one answered. Mother sucked in a long, deep breath and wiped her hands on the front of her skirt. She kept her gaze on her skirt. "When will she be here, Thomas?"

"It looks as though she'll arrive by train within a week."

"Nice of Edward to give you an option," Mother said through clenched teeth.

"Now, Lavina."

This time she held up her hand. "I know, I know. Just let me have a moment of self-pity to get used to the idea."

Father walked over to her and pulled her to her feet. He placed his arms around her waist. "Lavina, if ever there is a woman who forgives, it's you. It's your gift. Besides, it's not Eliza's fault her pa is the way he is."

Mother seemed to melt in Father's arms. "You're right. We'll make her welcome, Thomas, because she's family and because God loves us even when we don't deserve it."

Father smiled. "I love you, Lavina O'Connor."

Abigail quietly stepped out of the room, giving her parents a moment of privacy. The love between them had always made her feel secure. Eliza had probably never known that kind of security with a pa like Uncle Edward. Despite their differences in their childhood days, Abigail decided she would do what she could to make Eliza feel welcome.

❧

A knock sounded at the door. Abigail looked up from her novel. Barnabas barked and ran toward the sound. She put a marker in her book and walked over to answer the door. Pulling on the knob, she was surprised to see her best friend standing at the entrance.

"Sophia!" she exclaimed, reaching over to hug her. "Come in."

The two walked into the drawing room, Barnabas prancing at their feet. "So, you're the wonder dog I've been hearing so much about," Sophia said with a laugh as she settled into her seat. She pulled off her gloves and let Barnabas sniff her hands. When he finished, she tousled his hair. He seemed to lose interest in the visit, ambled over to Abigail, circled three times, then plopped in a heap at her feet. They both laughed.

"How is the little mother doing?" Abigail asked, looking at Sophia's growing midsection.

"I'm doing fine. The sickness has subsided, so things are looking up."

"Oh, Sophia, how are you?" Mother entered the room and gave Sophia a hug.

"I'm fine, thank you."

"How would you ladies like some tea?"

"That would be nice," Sophia answered.

"Thanks," Abigail agreed.

In the blink of an eye, Mother was out of the room, with the sound of clanging dishes coming from the kitchen.

"I hope you don't mind I stopped by. Since I haven't been able to make it to church as much lately, I had to see for myself how you were getting along." Sophia flashed a look of concern toward Abigail.

"You mean without Jonathan?"

Sophia nodded.

"I'm fine, really. I mean, I miss him, but I'm getting along all right." Abigail shrugged. "Just wasn't meant to be."

"What about your chauffeur?" Sophia asked with raised eyebrows. "He seems like a good catch."

"You and Gramma!" Abigail said with a laugh. She shook her head. "I'm not sure I want another relationship. I'm happy with my work at Barnabas House, and—"

"You don't want another relationship? Of course you do! My child has to have a playmate!"

They both laughed. Mother brought in the tea and handed a cup and saucer to each one.

"Tell her, Mrs. O'Connor," Sophia encouraged. "Tell her she has to find someone and get married soon so my child will have a playmate."

The older woman smiled and shook her head. "I've learned long ago once Abigail's mind is made up, I'm hard-pressed to change it." She threw a wink at Abigail and started to leave the room. Turning, she looked at Sophia. "But you're more than welcome to try." She laughed and went back to the kitchen.

"What about this Christopher you told me about at Barnabas House? Any chance of something with him?"

Abigail smiled. "Christopher is a wonderful friend, but it's not like that."

Sophia sipped her tea. "Well, the way I view it, you have two handsome men in your life, and you just can't throw away good prospects. I can see I'm going to have to pray harder."

Abigail groaned before taking a sip of tea. "How's your ma and Mrs. Baird?"

Sophia chuckled. "Mrs. Baird is ornery as always."

Abigail laughed and nodded.

"It's all Mama can do to keep up with her."

Abigail could hear the affection in Sophia's voice for the women. And rightfully so. They were both easy to love. "She has a lot of energy; I'll give her that." They paused a moment. "Still keeping busy sewing?"

Sophia nodded, put her cup in the saucer, and placed them on a nearby stand. "Do you remember Marie Zimmerman?"

"Uh-huh."

"She still helps me. I don't know what I'd do without her."

"How is her husband—wasn't it Seth?"

Sophia nodded. "He found a job with the railroad. They've managed to move out of the shanty and into a fine little cottage and are doing well. Their girls love school."

Abigail smiled, thinking of the little girls. "They are so cute." She took another drink of her tea.

Sophia looked into the distance. "I love those two." She absently rubbed her stomach.

Abigail looked at her and laughed. She put her teacup on the table, then turned to Sophia. "I can't believe you're married and expecting your first child! Where does the time go?"

Sophia shrugged and smiled. "I don't know."

"So, tell me about you and Clayton."

Sophia nodded with a sparkle in her eye. "I never knew I could be so happy, Abigail."

Abigail smiled. "I know. I can see it in you. You practically glow!" A comfortable silence followed. "His business is going well then?"

"Yes. And his father and mother are doing well."

"You've been very blessed." Abigail looked away for a moment.

"It will happen for you one day, Abby. If not with Jonathan, then with someone else God has in mind for you."

Abigail shrugged. "It doesn't matter."

"Don't give up. There are eligible men out there besides Jonathan Clark."

"I suppose."

They each drank some more of the tea while Mother answered another knock at the door.

"You know," Sophia said, "it's all so exciting. Why, the man of your dreams could walk through that door at any moment!"

No sooner had the words left Sophia's mouth than Titus appeared in the doorway. "Abigail?"

Her head jerked up with a start. With teacup still in hand, her sudden movement caused it to rattle on the saucer, sloshing the hot liquid about.

"Oh, I'm sorry," he said, hat in hand.

Sophia and Abigail exchanged a glance.

"What can I do for you, Titus?"

"I wanted to see when you would be heading for Barnabas House so I could have the carriage ready."

Sophia chimed in, a smile on her face. "I really need to be going anyway. We'll visit again soon," she was saying, already on her feet.

Titus looked to Abigail.

"I'll be ready in ten minutes."

He gave a quick nod and left. Sophia looked back at Abigail, and they both burst into laughter.

six

The weekend passed much too swiftly for Abigail. The children had most of their homework caught up, leaving her little to do at Barnabas House. Deciding to leave early, she asked Titus to take her to visit Gramma. She needed to see how Gramma was faring.

Once they arrived at Gramma's, Titus helped Abigail and Barnabas from the carriage. With his leash trailing behind him, Barnabas ran to the front door, barked a couple of times, then scurried over to a tree for a good sniffing.

Though Abigail was put out by Barnabas's moment of freedom, she laughed with Titus at her dog's antics. Upon hearing the creak of the front door, they turned to see Gramma standing at the entrance in a sensible gray dress. Titus stayed near the carriage and lifted his hand in greeting.

"Good day to ye," Gramma said, embracing Abigail at the door and nodding to Titus. "Come in, come in." Abigail stepped through the door. Barnabas rushed in behind her just before Gramma closed the door. Abigail made her way toward the sofa and settled in. Paws and leash clinking lightly against the wooden floor, Barnabas strolled up beside her and snuggled at her feet. Abigail gave a token scolding to the independent hound, then patted him for reassurance. Gramma opened the door again and called, "Ye come join us, laddie."

A scuffle sounded at the step, and Abigail turned in surprise to see Titus in the doorway. He fingered his hat as he talked. "I don't mean to intrude, ma'am."

" 'Tis no intrusion. No intrusion at all," Gramma said with a brush of her hand. "Please, come in." She turned back to Abigail and winked.

Abigail sighed and shook her head. Gramma was up to her

frolics again. Abigail looked at Titus, and he smiled, throwing her a what-could-I-do look. They settled down to tea.

After Gramma gleaned every bit of information out of Titus that she could possibly gather, she proceeded to list Abigail's attributes. By the time Gramma had finished her little speech, Abigail thought herself a saint by Gramma's standards.

"Enough of this, Gramma. You're making me blush."

Gramma shrugged. "So ye add a little color to ye face, aye?"

Titus walked over to her piano. "May I?" he asked.

A pleasurable smile lit Gramma's face as she nodded her approval.

Titus scooted onto the piano bench and began to play some classical themes that Abigail had heard before but whose titles she didn't know. She closed her eyes and listened, letting the music lift her from her fatigue and stress of the day and carry her to a place of comfort. Once the last note faded, she lingered a moment longer, then opened her eyes.

Gramma's eyes, alight with sparkle like she had stumbled upon a well-kept secret, stared at her. The expression on Gramma's face brought Abigail to her senses. She turned to Titus, who was also looking her way. "It's beautiful, Titus. Where did you learn to play like that?"

He shrugged. "Ma taught me. She used to be quite the pianist and occasionally helped out at Hooley's Opera House."

Abigail found the information intriguing. She didn't know that about Titus. But then, she didn't know much about him at all.

He turned in his seat and started another tune. "Amazing Grace." This one she knew; she hummed the melody, then started singing the words. Before they knew it, beautiful music filled the air. They passed the hour playing and singing such tunes as "Buffalo Gals," "Oh! Susanna," "Jim Crack Corn," "Jeanie with the Light Brown Hair," song after song until they were finally spent.

They laughed and visited awhile longer, then decided they had to leave.

"This afternoon ye have brought great joy to this tired heart, that ye have," Gramma said, cupping Abigail's face in her hands. Gramma kissed Abigail's cheek, then turned to Titus. "And ye, laddie. I'll be thanking ye for the fine music."

Titus's face lit up. The smile that stretched across his face made Abigail's heart flip, startling her. They turned and walked out the door, Barnabas following close behind. Once they reached the carriage, Titus stopped and looked at Abigail for a fleeting moment. Her pulse drummed hard against her ears. Neither said a word. Yet their silence spoke volumes.

❧

Titus led the horses through the streets as dusk crept into the sky. He took off his hat and shoved his fingers through his hair. What had gotten into him? He couldn't let this woman get under his skin. He had a job to do. Abigail and the O'Connors were muddling everything. Why did they treat him like family? He wanted to think it was their guilt, but deep down, he knew such a burden didn't drive them. Their faith made them care about others. Not just him. They weren't doing good for appearance's sake. They lived a "life of thankfulness," as Mr. O'Connor had put it, for what God had done for them. That knowledge pricked him. Why couldn't God do things for him, too? Why did God take his pa? Why did God strip Titus of his dream to one day be a doctor?

By the time the horses arrived at Abigail's home, he had worked himself up good. He wanted no part of that woman. Keep his distance—that's what he'd do. No more letting her rattle him with her gentle smile, the sparkle in her eyes, and her kind ways. No, he had to stand firm, find what he needed to bring them down, and get on with his life.

He jumped off his carriage seat and helped Abigail down, his jaw taut, teeth clenched. She smiled, then upon seeing his face quickly lowered her eyes. "Thank you," she whispered before heading for the door.

He felt like a heel, a scoundrel. She didn't deserve his treatment, but he couldn't stop now. He'd come too far. The

O'Connor family had to pay. He'd suffered too much.

Unhitching the team from the carriage, his thoughts rambled on when he was struck with an idea. He would go to their church and see what he could find out, see what made them tick, so he'd know better how to bring them down. Putting the horses back in their stalls, he decided that's what he'd do.

Come Sunday, he would go to church.

◆

Abigail went straight to her room. She had had a wonderful afternoon, but what just happened out in the stable? One minute Titus seemed wonderful, and the next, well, she didn't know what to think.

She laid across the bed, but Barnabas whined from the floor. "Oh, you!" she said, pulling herself up to console him. "I'm the one who needs a kind pat or two, not you."

Barnabas seemed to ignore her completely. Abigail continued to comfort her dog while thinking of Titus. Where had his thoughts taken him during the carriage ride? Was he afraid she would read more into their afternoon than was there? Perhaps he had another young lady in his life. She gasped, causing Barnabas to look up. Until that very moment, she hadn't thought of that possibility.

Abigail heaved a big sigh and plopped back on her bed again. As long as she lived, she would never understand men. One minute you felt quite sure they were smitten; the next minute, their attention was focused fully on newspapers, horses, or who knew what.

Maybe when her cousin arrived, she and Abigail could share secrets. Some cousins were close like that. Abigail hoped they could be. Of course, Sophia was her best friend. Still, it would be nice to have a cousin with a shared spirit. Kind of like having a sister.

Her mind replayed the afternoon's events. Titus playing on the piano, the look in Gramma's eyes. The look of affection filled Titus's eyes when he watched her from the piano. She hadn't missed it. It warmed her clear through.

Thoughts of Jonathan had grown fewer with every passing day. Perhaps she had moved on without him. Much sooner than she had expected. Quite possibly she didn't love him after all. That revelation surprised her.

Then another thought came to her, surprising her even more. Perhaps she could give love one more chance.

❧

"Where are you going?" Ma asked.

"I'm going to church," Titus said matter-of-factly.

Ma looked like she would faint dead away. "Where are you going to church?"

"I'm going to the O'Connors' church."

Her eyes narrowed. "Why the sudden interest?"

He shrugged.

Ma's eyes turned big as coins. A smile broke out on her face. "It's Abigail, isn't it?"

"No, it's not Abigail. I just want to go."

"Oh, Son, you don't have to hide your feelings. I think she's a lovely young lady."

"Ma, it's not Abigail," he barked. One look at her face made him feel bad for his tone. "I'm sorry, Ma. I'm just going to church. That's all."

Her expression grew serious. "Titus, you watch yourself."

"Don't worry, Ma."

She walked over to him and kissed his cheek. "Don't let hate rule you, Son. I love you. I don't want to lose you, too." Before he could answer, she turned and busied herself with breakfast preparations.

Jenny smiled at him. "What are you smiling about?" he teased, tousling her hair. For a moment, his heart pricked. He was doing this for Jenny, too. After all, she was affected by what the O'Connors did to them. He justified his actions, cleaning his heart of any trace of guilt. After breakfast, he gave Jenny a kiss on the head, then did the same to Ma. "I'll see you later."

He walked through the door, barely hearing Ma's words that she was still praying for him.

&

Titus walked into church with the O'Connor family. His boots scuffed the wooden floors. It had been awhile since he'd darkened the doors of such a place. The building was small, not at all like what he had imagined. Every eye seemed to turn and look at him, making him uncomfortable. The boards groaned when they finally settled onto the rough-hewn benches. Titus took great care as he scooted across the worn and splintered bench.

The reverend, somewhat familiar in his approach to the people, surprised Titus. He liked it, though. Oh, there he went again. Getting his mind off of his reason for being there. This wasn't a real church visit. He was there for one reason: to find out how to bring down the O'Connor family.

The reverend's sermon spoke of forgiveness. Of course. What else? Ma was praying. She did this to him. Though he loved her, sometimes she made him want to spit. He often wondered if she had a direct line to God. Seemed God answered all of her prayers.

Well, maybe not all. Had Ma prayed about their current situation? Surely Ma had prayed about Jenny. Where was God in all that?

Titus shifted in his seat and refocused on the reverend's words. He talked of David's forgiveness toward his enemy Saul. Of all the things to talk about. Hadn't Titus already rehashed those stories in his mind? The reverend reminded them that though Saul had made several attempts on David's life, David stayed true to God. He would not touch the Lord's anointed.

Well, Titus could rest easy. The O'Connors were not the Lord's anointed. Were they? What did that mean, anyway? Someone chosen of God? To do what, preach? Saul wasn't a preacher, but a king. The O'Connors wouldn't fit. God understood Titus's feelings. God would approve.

He had to.

❧

Church was over faster than the flutter of a hummingbird's wings, and Titus had little time to mingle with the people to find out anything on the O'Connors. It would take time, no doubt. He'd have to be patient. Still, he didn't want to risk too much time. He didn't like the way his heart turned over at the sight of Abigail. The sooner he could leave their home, the better.

"You will join us for lunch, Titus?" Mrs. O'Connor asked.

He looked at Abigail. "Oh yes, and you have to play me in checkers," she encouraged. "But I'll warn you, I'm good."

His eyebrows lifted. "Oh, a challenge? Well, I don't see how I can refuse." He turned to Mrs. O'Connor. "I'll be there." He mentally kicked himself. What was he thinking? He wasn't. The words were out of his mouth before he had time to think.

After a meal of beef, potatoes, corn, and biscuits, Titus and Abigail settled into a game of checkers in front of the hearth. Barnabas lay coiled at her feet. Over the next hour, they played a couple of games, stopping to chat between moves, each winning one game. Titus insisted on a third to break the tie. Abigail took up the challenge, and much to his pleasure, Titus won. Abigail gave in agreeably; then Mr. O'Connor invited Titus to a game of chess.

Titus couldn't remember when he'd passed such an enjoyable afternoon. He only wished it hadn't been with the O'Connors. Oh, he was learning more about them, all right, but he was learning things he didn't want to know. Like the fact that they seemed genuine. He hadn't expected that. He had thought they would be like most people who claimed religion. Fake. Yet this family was different. They actually believed what they said they believed. Made him almost sorry he didn't share in their faith.

Before leaving, Titus edged his way out to the barn to check on the horses. Although it was his day off, he had grown to care about the animals and wanted to see to them.

"They kind of grow on you, don't they?" Mr. O'Connor's voice came from behind Titus.

Titus turned to him and smiled. "Yeah, I guess they do at that."

"Look, Titus, you've done a good job for us, and I want to thank you." Mr. O'Connor waited a moment. "There's something else." Titus looked up at him. "I've never told you how sorry I was about your pa. He was a good friend. I never meant for him to. . .well, I. . ." Tears welled up in the older man's face, confusing Titus. This was all wrong. He didn't want to see genuine concern on his enemy's face. This man was his enemy. Titus did not want to care about him or his family. Titus turned away.

"I didn't know he had put everything into that business, or I would have tried to stop him."

Titus turned back to him. Mr. O'Connor placed a hand on Titus's shoulder. "I want to help you, Titus, because I know your pa would have done the same for my family had the tables been turned."

Titus was speechless. What could he say? His thoughts warred. He wanted to. . .

Get even.

Before his heart could thaw, Titus fought back, allowing the chill to return, cold and hard like icicles. He said nothing.

Mr. O'Connor looked into Titus's eyes and paused. Without a word, he patted Titus on the shoulder, then turned and walked away.

seven

Shaking the snow from her boots, Abigail stepped into Barnabas House and pulled off her cloak. She thought it best to keep Barnabas at home today since it was so cold. A pleasurable smell of stew meandered from the kitchen through the front room to greet her. As she hung her cloak on a nearby peg, she glanced at the freshly painted white walls. It hardly seemed to Abigail the same place as when she first started working there.

She walked over to the fireplace to warm herself a moment. Her cheeks were still stinging from the biting cold, but she felt refreshed, invigorated, and ready to work. Winter did that to her. Rubbing her hands in front of the open fire, she spoke greetings to a few of the workers. A movement in the window caught her attention. Outside, delicate snowflakes fluttered to the ground, reminding Abigail of a scene from Currier and Ives. With a happy sigh, she pulled herself away and headed toward her table to work with the children.

"Abigail, how are you?"

She turned with a start to see Christopher standing there. "Oh, hello! I'm so glad you're better."

A huge smile spread across his face. "That makes two of us." He looked around the room. "I've missed this place. And I'm so thankful you and the others were able to keep it going while I was gone. Thanks, too, for organizing the painting. The place looks nice."

"Well, Mary O'Grady did most of the organizing. She worked hard to keep things going while you were gone."

Christopher's eyes sparkled. "That woman is a wonder."

Abigail thought she heard something in his voice. Admiration? No, it was more than that. Definitely more. Her face must have revealed her thoughts.

Christopher cleared his throat. "Well, it's hard to believe here it is December tenth already. Christmas will soon be upon us."

Abigail smiled, then turned giddy with the thought of Christmas. She loved Christmas with all the trimmings and festivities the holiday brought.

"I see you like this time of year."

"Yes, I love it."

"Miss Abigail, I have something for you." Katie O'Grady tugged at Abigail's dress. She held something behind her back.

Abigail looked down at her and smiled. The sight of the child brought out her maternal instincts. "Is that a fact?" she asked, looking at Katie.

Katie beamed and nodded with vigor.

"Well, I'll leave you two for now," Christopher said with a wink.

"Thank you, Christopher," Abigail returned, then scrunched down in front of Katie. One thing about it: Mary O'Grady might be poor, but her daughter's face was as shiny as a scrubbed apple. Hems had been dropped on her two dresses and tears mended. "Now, what is it you wanted to show me?"

"Could we go over there?" Katie pointed to a vacant corner out of the way of others.

Abigail smiled. "Certainly." Together they scuffled through the busy room, across the wooden floor, and hunkered in the corner as if sharing a wonderful secret.

"This is my favorite necklace. I wore it every day until Bobby broke it." Katie's eyes filled with tears as she stretched out her hand. "I want to give it to you." There in her delicate palm lay a golden locket with a broken chain.

Abigail gasped. "Why, Katie, I could not take such a wonderful gift from you. Where did you get it?"

"Ma gave it to me. It don't have her picture, though. She didn't have one." Katie opened the locket and showed an empty shell where a picture should have been.

"You cannot give away such a precious gift, Katie. Your ma meant that for you."

She lifted worried eyes to Abigail. A look that said she wanted to give her best gift, yet didn't want to part with such a treasure. "Ma said when you love someone, you give them your best gift, just like God did when He gave His Son, Jesus." All wiggles and energy, she couldn't seem to stand still but moved about and scratched as new itches seemed to surface. "I know it's broke, but it's still my favorite thing." Suddenly, she pulled herself straight, squaring her shoulders as if she were about to recite a memory verse word for word. "Ma said broken things could be fixed. But only God can fix a broken heart." She snapped her head and grinned at her own delivery of the speech.

Abigail felt a squeeze on her heart. No doubt Mary O'Grady still ached over her husband's abandonment and death. Abigail's pain over losing Jonathan was nothing compared to what this woman had suffered.

Katie swayed in half circles as she talked to Abigail. Her hands waved with her words. "Ma says I have to forgive Bobby for breaking my necklace just like she has to forgive Pa for leaving us," she said matter-of-factly. She stopped and licked her lips very slowly, like she was tasting honey from a biscuit. Raising her right arm, she swiped her wet mouth with the back of her hand. "I'm still mad at him, though." As if someone pushed a button, her eyebrows crinkled at the same time her lower lip jutted out. "Ma says she'll pray for me." She frowned and stared at the necklace in her hand and lifted teary eyes to Abigail. "Don't you like my gift, Miss Abigail?"

"Oh!" Abigail pulled the child into an enormous hug. When they finally separated, Abigail looked into Katie's green eyes. "Katie, I love your present."

With only a slight hesitation, Katie dropped the precious locket and broken chain into Abigail's waiting hand. Abigail knew Katie had sacrificed her most treasured gift. "Thank you."

The little girl's face brightened, and her tears dried. Without another word, Katie skipped over to the table where she worked on her homework, and no doubt the entire scene was quickly forgotten. But Abigail knew she would never forget the sacrificial gift given to her by a pink-cheeked little Irish girl on a chilly winter's afternoon.

☙

Sunday morning, Titus walked behind Abigail as they made their way out of the church. He found himself spending more time with the O'Connors than necessary but couldn't seem to turn them down when they invited him. As much as he hated to admit it, he enjoyed their company. His plan gnawed at him, but he pushed it aside for now. It didn't hurt to enjoy life a little, did it? He'd get back to his plan, but for now, he wanted to spend a little more time with Abigail.

"Abigail!"

Titus was just helping Abigail into the carriage when they heard her name. They both turned to see Sophia and Clayton coming toward them.

"Oh, I was hoping to catch you before you left," Sophia said, somewhat out of breath.

"Titus," Clayton said with a grin, extending his hand.

"Good to see you again, Clayton."

"Well, I wanted to know if you and Titus could join us for lunch." Sophia looked hopeful. Abigail hesitated a moment, then looked at Titus as if she feared what he might say or think.

"It's fine with me," he said.

Abigail visibly relaxed. A smile lifted her lips. "We'd like that. Let me tell Mother."

"Good," Sophia said with a snap of her head. "We'll see you there."

Titus turned to Abigail. "You'd have to ride with me in my buckboard since your parents will need the carriage."

She smiled, putting all his fear to rest. "That will be fine."

Somehow he knew she meant it, too.

Her parents gave their blessing. Titus and Abigail waved good-bye and headed toward Sophia and Clayton's home. He felt a little self-conscious being a mere chauffeur with Clayton an attorney and all. He reminded himself these people didn't seem to care in the least. So why should he?

Titus pulled the buffalo skin up from the wagon, brushed it off, and gave it to Abigail. "Here, you'll need this."

"Thanks," she said, adjusting it around her to ward off the biting chill.

Soft white flakes filled the air as they traveled the roads to Sophia and Clayton's country home. Meadows once filled with wildflowers lay in frigid heaps, waiting for spring's thaw.

"I'm sorry it's cold. But at least it's pretty to look at, don't you think?"

Abigail smiled with pure pleasure. "I'm glad to find someone else besides me who loves the season. I was beginning to think the world was full of grouses."

Titus laughed. His eyebrows quirked and lowered. "I guess I'm not a grouse, at least when it comes to winter."

Abigail studied him for a minute, making him feel a little uncomfortable. "So tell me about your ma."

His spirit dropped. He didn't want to talk about his family. That was too personal. They were stepping into intimate territory. Yet it was a perfectly sound question. After all, he'd spent lots of time with her family. He decided to answer.

"Ma's amazing. Her spirits are always up, despite the circumstances."

"I'm sorry about everything, Titus. I know things haven't been easy for you."

The sincerity of her words tugged at him in ways he didn't want to explore. "The main thing is to get Jenny walking—and talking again."

"Oh, I knew she didn't walk, but I didn't realize she couldn't talk."

"Just since Pa died. She talked before then."

"Oh, how awful. I'm so sorry."

"We'll get by," he said, scratching his jaw. He just didn't want to tell her he had to take her family down to bring his family peace. His heart constricted. The truth was he was getting soft. Second-guessing himself. Abigail seemed to sense his inner struggle. She kept silent the rest of the journey.

❧

"Abigail, you must see what I've made for the baby," Sophia said, placing the soup ladle on the stove. Grabbing Abigail's hand, Sophia took her friend to the bedroom. She bent down in front of her trunk.

"Oh, Sophia, your mother gave you the trunk?"

Sophia looked up, beaming. "You remember?"

"How could I forget? That's the one Clayton found in the fire, right?"

"Right." Sophia ran her fingers along the top of the trunk. "Papa's gift to Mama, Clayton's gift to me." She lifted the lid almost as if there were something sacred inside. Carefully, she picked up a knitted yellow blanket, woven in an intricate pattern.

Abigail gasped. "Oh my, Sophia, you knitted this?"

Sophia smiled with pride. "Do you like it?"

Abigail held it tenderly, pressing it softly against her face. "It is beautiful." She handed the blanket back to Sophia. "Your baby is very blessed to have you and Clayton for parents."

"We are the ones most blessed," she corrected, slipping the blanket gingerly back into the trunk. She closed the lid and looked to Abigail. "Do you still miss him?"

"Who?"

Sophia laughed. "Well, I guess that answers my question."

"Oh, you mean Jonathan?"

Sophia nodded, her eyes probing.

"Only a little. It's not so bad now."

"You never hear from him?"

Abigail shook her head. "It's all right. I've moved on."

"I can see that," Sophia said, nodding her head toward the door with a laugh.

"No, no. I don't mean that."

"Titus is handsome, don't you think?"

"There you go again."

"Well?"

"All right, he's handsome, but I'm not ready for another relationship, Sophia. Really."

Sophia studied her a moment. "You will be one day. I hope Titus is still around." She pulled herself up from her knees and walked through the door, but her words lingered in the room with Abigail.

❧

When the women walked into the room, Abigail overheard Titus talking to Clayton about his dream of becoming a doctor. Her heart ached as she heard the longing in his voice. Dreams obliterated. She wished there was something she could do to help him get back to medical school. His mother had her hands full taking care of Jenny. He was their sole provider. How could he possibly come up with money or time for medical school?

Titus turned to see her looking at him. He stopped talking. Clayton seemed to notice the awkward moment. "How's the soup coming, Sophia? This man is hungry," he said with a laugh.

"It's almost ready."

Abigail placed the dishes on the table, and soon they gathered around for prayer and eating. Sophia scooped ample portions of steaming stew into hefty bowls. The sight of the stew, thick with vegetables, made Abigail's stomach growl. She could hardly wait to eat. Sophia's mother had taught her daughter well in the art of cooking.

By the time lunch was over and the afternoon spent, the snow had subsided. Abigail and Titus said their good-byes to Sophia and Clayton and headed home just before dusk.

"Thank you, Titus, for coming along. I hope it didn't make you uncomfortable to be paired with me today." Feeling her words were too forward, Abigail almost wished she hadn't spoken them.

He looked at her and smiled. "I didn't mind it at all. I had a wonderful time." His eyes locked with hers long enough to make her heart skip. She pulled her gaze away, not daring to dwell on what was happening between them.

They traveled the way home in comfortable silence. Abigail found herself wishing Titus didn't have to leave. When he drew the buckboard in front of her home, he turned to her. He looked like he wanted to say something. He leaned in, and she lost her breath, feeling quite sure he was about to kiss her, but before she could react, he pulled away and jumped out of the buckboard. He came over to her side and helped her out, walking her to the door. "Good night, Abigail," he said without looking.

Befuddled, she watched as he quickly boarded his wagon and headed home.

She watched him leave. "What was that all about?" The wind lifted her words into the night air, but the question remained upon her heart.

eight

Wednesday morning, Titus stood in the drawing room of the O'Connor home, circling his hat between his fingers. "Sorry to keep you waiting, Titus," Abigail said, lifting her bag. An abundance of volunteers at Barnabas House had left her with fewer hours to work. She hadn't talked to Titus since their afternoon at Clayton and Sophia's on Sunday. She felt a little nervous talking to him since their last meeting, wondering what was going on inside of him. Without saying a word, he shoved his hat on his head, and they turned to leave.

Before they left the drawing room, a knock sounded. Barnabas barked and ran through the hallway, skidding to a halt at the front door.

Mother's footsteps sounded in the hallway. "I'll get it."

While they waited a moment, Abigail felt anxious to fill the silence. "How have you been this week, Titus?"

He lifted his gaze to her. "I've been fine. How about you?"

"Good." An awkward moment stretched between them. Titus looked like he wanted to say more. If only she could read him. He filled the gap with talk of the horses. Ignoring Barnabas's warning barks of a stranger in the house, they slid into a comfortable discussion. So lost were they in conversation that when Mother entered the room, it took them completely by surprise.

Abigail looked up to see an attractive, blond-haired woman, dressed in the latest fashions and colors, standing beside Mother. The woman tilted her chin and seemed to look Abigail over as if she were a bolt of cloth. It unnerved her a little.

"Abigail, it's been awhile since you've seen her, but this is your cousin Eliza."

Abigail felt her stomach plunge. Most likely a response brought on from years gone by. *Let it go, Abigail*, she told herself. Eliza walked over to Abigail, extending her hand. "Hello. You haven't changed a bit," she said with a sugary whine. "Same freckles and—" Eliza's gaze ran over Abigail. "Well, everything."

Somehow Abigail felt the comment was meant to dig under her skin.

It did.

Eliza O'Connor. With the same personality as Abigail had remembered. "And I see you haven't changed," Abigail said, all the while noticing Eliza didn't appear the sickly cousin that Uncle Edward had described in his letter. They shook hands rather awkwardly.

Eliza turned to Titus and gave him a look that made Abigail blush. Before Mother could introduce them, Eliza stepped up to him. "And you are. . . ?" she asked with obvious interest.

Titus took a step back. "Um, Titus Matthews, ma'am," he said, tipping his hat.

A sly smile curved the corners of her mouth. "I like that name," she said with unreserved boldness.

Mother coughed, seemingly taken aback by Eliza's behavior. "Titus is our friend and our chauffeur."

Eliza's eyebrows rose as she seemed to consider this information, then she smiled again. "I'll look forward to a pleasant carriage ride then," she said, eyes twinkling.

Abigail's jaw dropped in astonishment, never before having seen such a lavish display of feminine daring.

"Will you be staying at Barnabas House all day, Abigail?" Mother wanted to know.

Abigail clamped her mouth shut, swallowed, then looked at her mother. "No, I won't be working with the children today, so I'm going over long enough to help Christopher with a few things, and I'll be back around eleven o'clock."

"Good," Mother said. "I'll plan on lunch around then." She

turned to Titus. "You'll join us today, Titus, or do you have other plans?"

He cleared his throat. "Um, I'm beholden to you, Mrs. O'Connor."

"Good. Lunch at eleven o'clock," she said with a snap of her head. She turned to Eliza. "That will give you time to get settled in your room and freshen up, if you so desire."

Eliza turned to Titus. Her eyes never leaving his face, she responded, "I do so desire to freshen up. A lady must always look her best." She threw a delicate smile his way, then turned to Abigail. "Isn't that right, Cousin?"

Abigail's cheeks flamed, no doubt giving Eliza the answer she sought. Eliza laughed and followed Mother to the stairway, leaving Abigail speechless.

❧

Arriving home from Barnabas House, Abigail pulled her wraps tighter around her neck, making her way from the barn to the house. The winter winds had picked up, biting into her face. She looked at the heavy clouds overhead, noting snow would most likely cover the ground by evening.

Once inside, she pushed hard on the front door to shut out the cold. Barnabas yapped at her feet until she finally reached down and paid attention to him. "I'm sorry you didn't get to go today. Maybe next time," she said to the lovable hound as he scooted around so she could scratch every possible itch. Once she felt sure he was satisfied with the reassuring rubs and words of greeting, Abigail tugged at her scarf and headed toward her room. Before she could reach the stairs, her mother came through the drawing room and stepped into the hallway.

"Abigail, glad you're home, dear. I hate to do this, but before you take off your wraps, would you let Titus know that lunch is ready?"

Abigail smiled. "Certainly." Mother turned to go, and Abigail pushed her scarf back in place, bracing herself for the cold winds.

Once at the barn, Abigail poked her head around the stall. "Titus?"

He stepped from the shadows toward her. "Yeah?"

"Oh," Abigail said with a laugh, "you startled me. Mother wanted me to tell you lunch is ready."

"Thanks. I'll be there in a second."

She nodded and walked away. Knowing Eliza would join them for lunch, Abigail couldn't help wondering how Titus felt about her cousin.

≈

Titus put the hay in a corner and brushed the fragments from his hands. He wondered why the O'Connors allowed him to eat with them. After all, he was merely their servant. The idea burned him. Yet he couldn't deny they had been very kind to him. Too kind. He didn't like it. Constantly, he had to remind himself their goodness stemmed from a guilty conscience. Why else would they treat him like he was one of the family?

With deliberate steps, he made his way toward the house. In a weak moment, he had to admit their kindness made his job all the more difficult. How could he burn with hate toward people who reached out to him? He mentally shook himself. All of a sudden, he found himself getting soft, and he didn't like it. Weak. Next thing he knew, he'd be using God as a crutch. . . .

Once inside the house, they gathered around the table, said the blessing, then passed the bowls. Titus tried to eat and get away from the table as soon as possible. Eliza stared at him most of the way through the meal, making him uncomfortable. He wasn't used to pushy womenfolk. It troubled him. She wasn't bad to look at, but something about her didn't ring right with him. He glanced at Abigail. She pushed the food around on her plate, not talking much, not eating much. He wondered why.

"Titus?" Mrs. O'Connor caught his attention.

"Yes, ma'am."

"We would like very much for you and your family to join us for Christmas."

He looked at her with a start. "I. . .uh, I. . ."

She shook her head. "Now, we won't take no for an answer. You have them here at about noon for Christmas dinner." Mrs. O'Connor winked at him and continued with her meal. He looked at Abigail, who blushed beneath his stare. Then he glanced at Eliza, who seemed put out about something. Yet once she realized she had his attention, she smiled sweetly.

Mrs. O'Connor started talking about how nice it was to have Eliza in their home. He looked at Eliza again. She rolled her eyes, as if totally bored with her aunt's and Abigail's company. Somehow he knew that didn't include him. She made sure to throw plenty of other signals his way. The sooner he could get back to the stables, the better.

Horses were much easier to contend with than women.

⁂

After lunch, Abigail plopped on her bed. Barnabas jumped up and nudged her hand with his nose. She stroked him as she allowed her thoughts to wander. What had gotten into her? She saw the way Eliza looked at Titus. Surely he had noticed, too. What Abigail couldn't understand was why that bothered her. So what if Eliza and Titus were attracted to one another? Why should Abigail care?

Barnabas padded over the plump covers and finally curled into a ball at the foot of the bed. Abigail threw herself back on the bed and stared at the ceiling. True, she and Titus had become friends. After all, they were together every day, going on some errand or another. Perhaps she was being protective of him, knowing Eliza's true character.

She scolded herself. Maybe she didn't know Eliza's true character. Abigail didn't want to jump to conclusions because of her cousin's comments upon first meeting. It was quite possible Eliza was sincere in her remarks. Abigail couldn't deny, though, the obvious sneer in Eliza's voice. She was like a dog marking territory.

A knock sounded on her bedroom door. Eliza's voice called, "Abigail?"

Abigail jumped up from the bed, stopped a moment at the looking glass and fussed with her hair, then walked over to the door and opened it.

"Are we going to visit Gramma O'Connor this afternoon?"

"Yes. I'll just get my things." Abigail turned to gather her bag. Eliza stepped into the room and looked around. "How quaint. My quilt print was much the same as yours before I got a more fashionable one. I always liked that *old* quilt, though," she said, as if looking into years long gone.

Abigail seethed. Of all the nerve! It wasn't as if her bedroom furnishings were all that old. Besides, it didn't matter. She liked them. Her chin lifted. She would not let Eliza's meanness get to her.

Eliza raised her gaze to meet Abigail's. A knowing smirk played on her lips. Eliza would like nothing more than to get under Abigail's skin. Not wanting to give Eliza the satisfaction, Abigail offered a smile before walking through the doorway. "We'd best be going."

Hearing Eliza's dress swish along the floor in an effort to keep up made Abigail feel better. Her feet padded along at a stress-driven pace.

"Titus will be taking us, right?" Eliza wanted to know.

"Of course. He's our chauffeur."

"And a mighty handsome one at that." Eliza had caught up with her now and peered at Abigail.

Abigail looked at her a moment and turned away.

"Come on, surely you've noticed?" Eliza insisted.

"Eliza, Titus Matthews's physical appearance is of no concern to me."

"Oh? Then he's fair game?" Her voice held a thin veil of challenge.

"Well. . ." Abigail didn't know what to say. Finally, she lifted her chin. "Yes. Yes, of course."

Eliza flashed a victory smile. "Good."

They stepped through the front doorway into the flutter of falling snow, though Abigail couldn't help but feel they were heading into something much more ominous.

❧

Abigail and Eliza sipped on hot tea in Gramma's front room. Gramma shared wonderful stories of their fathers' childhood days, which kept Abigail on the edge of her seat. Eliza, on the other hand, drank her tea and worked on some needlework she had brought with her.

"That's a fine piece of needlework ye have there, Eliza."

For a moment, Abigail thought Eliza looked genuinely pleased. "I've worked with stitches for years," she finally announced, as if she wondered how they could think her work would be less than exquisite.

"So ye have finished your Christmas shopping, have ye?" Gramma asked, changing the subject from Eliza.

"I have everything done, but I was wondering if I should get something for Titus," Abigail said, searching Gramma's face.

Eliza's head jerked toward Abigail. "You're buying your chauffeur a present?" she asked, her eyes glaring.

"Well, I. . ." Abigail thought it had seemed a friendly gesture. After all, Titus was practically like one of the family.

Gramma came to the rescue. "Ah, 'tis a lovely idea, Abigail darling. The laddie is like ye family."

Eliza frowned at both of them. Her nose pointed upward. "It seems odd to me that a young lady should buy a present for her chauffeur, that's all," she said, lowering her gaze only long enough to stab her needle into the cloth she held and, with obvious irritation, yank the thread through to the other side.

Abigail thought it amusing that suddenly Eliza would concern herself with propriety.

Gramma ignored her comment and went on with another story about her sons, Thomas and Edward.

Midway through Gramma's story, Eliza turned to her cousin. "Abigail, shouldn't we be going? No doubt Titus is waiting on us by now."

Abigail was appalled at the un-Christian thoughts about this woman that assailed her mind. She threw an apologetic look to Gramma and looked back to Eliza. "I'm sure we can stay long enough for Gramma to finish her story." Her words held chastisement, and without blinking, Abigail kept her gaze locked with Eliza's.

Eliza tilted her head to one side and frowned at Gramma. "I thought you were finished." She began to put her needle-work materials in a bag.

Sorrow shadowed Gramma's face. Abigail wanted to hug her. She wanted to do something else to Eliza but refused to allow herself the luxury of lingering on that thought.

Gramma finished her story, although Abigail suspected Gramma had shortened it to please Eliza. " 'Tis time ye be going. I'll see ye on Christmas Day, then?"

Abigail stood and dropped a kiss on Gramma's cheek. "Yes, we'll look forward to it."

Without looking back, Eliza pranced across the floor and called, "Bye, Gramma," over her shoulder before disappearing through the door. Gramma and Abigail exchanged a glance, and Gramma gave her an extra squeeze. Abigail wondered how she would get through these days with her difficult cousin.

Stepping into the sunlight, Abigail's thoughts drifted to Christmas once again. If she'd had any doubts about getting Titus a present before, they were now gone. Feeling a trifle rebellious over her cousin's display of distaste toward the idea, Abigail suddenly thought a present for Titus seemed the perfect idea.

❧

The children could hardly concentrate on their studies as talk of Christmas filled the air. The workers had covered Barnabas House with Christmas greenery and holly. The smell of cider permeated the building, along with aromas of roasted chicken, potatoes, glazed carrots, applesauce, and cookies. Many kind folks had contributed to the Christmas lunch.

Abigail passed around candy to the children as her gift to them. Barnabas sported a handsome red bow around his neck, which made the children giggle at first sight. They decided he looked like a Christmas present, and everyone wanted to take him home. Abigail had to remind them he stayed with her but truly belonged to all of them. Barnabas strutted around the frolicking group, seeming quite pleased with all the attention.

Having alerted Mary O'Grady to what she was about to do, Abigail called Katie over to a quiet corner. "Katie, I have a special present for you." Mary watched from nearby.

The little girl's eyes grew wide, the light in them sparkling with excitement.

"Remember the very precious gift you gave to me?"

Katie nodded her head with all the energy of a six-year-old. "Well," Abigail continued, "here is what I have for you." An open locket holding Mary O'Grady's picture dangled from a new golden chain and dropped into Katie's chubby palm. It had taken some doing for Mary to find a picture for Abigail to place in the locket, but they finally came up with one. Abigail waited, holding her breath. She didn't want to offend Katie by giving back her gift, yet she knew how much the child had not wanted to part with it.

Katie gasped. Large tears toppled from her eyes and streaked down her plump cheeks. "That's Ma! And you fixed my broken chain!" Before Abigail could respond, Katie threw her arms around her and squeezed her tight. When Katie released her, she bit her lip for a moment. "But now you don't have a present."

"Ah, but I do, Katie. My gift is the pleasure of seeing your eyes when you looked upon your ma's picture and your special locket. I'll feel happy every time I see you wear it."

Katie hugged her once again. "Ma says the gift that brings the most pleasure is the one that is hardest to give." She wiped the tears from her face. "I didn't want to give you my special locket. But since it was the hardest to give, I knew you would like it most."

"Oh!" Abigail's words caught in her throat. She closed her eyes to the tears that sprang forth. Once she opened her eyes, she saw Mary O'Grady smiling and wiping tears from her own face.

If she never took another breath, Abigail knew Christmas had already come to her. For in that moment, she learned the most precious gift she had to give was her heart. And she understood that she must risk giving it away in a manner she had never done before.

One day. . .

nine

Abigail rubbed her eyes and opened them to the morning light that streamed through her windowpane. Outside, lacy snowflakes fell from a frosty sky to the ground below. A childish excitement swept through her like a December blizzard. Quickly she pulled on her slippers and robe, then ran to the window.

She turned to look at Barnabas who, with droopy eyes, watched her, all the while staying curled at the foot of her bed.

Abigail laughed and looked back out the window. With childish abandon, she thought herself in the most magical of places. She drank in the scene of frosted trees topped by an icing of snow and imagined the frost on the fence post was a smattering of fairy dust.

It was Christmas! The one day in all the year when she refused to be sad about anything.

Quickly dressing for the day, Abigail made her way into the kitchen, where she ate her breakfast.

Morning gave way to afternoon as Abigail worked alongside her mother with the meal preparations. Just when dinner was ready to serve, someone knocked at the front door.

"Oh, would you get that, Abigail?" Mother called from the kitchen.

Abigail went to the door and opened it. There stood Titus, holding his sister in his arms, his ma standing beside him, and Gramma beside her. "Oh, come in," Abigail said, hastily moving out of the way.

The little family went into the drawing room. Abigail pointed to a sofa, where Titus carefully laid his sister. After quick introductions, Titus took Jenny's cloak from her, as well as his own, and handed them to Abigail. Mrs. Matthews and Gramma did the same.

Abigail put the winter wraps away, then rejoined them. After a short visit, Mother announced the meal was ready and in no time at all, they were sitting around the dinner table. Father offered the prayer. Finally, the sounds of clanging silverware, bowls thumping against the wooden table, and soft chatter filled the room.

"Jenny, would you like some of this?" Abigail asked, pointing to the potatoes. The little girl nodded slightly and lifted a shy smile. One by one, Abigail found Jenny's preferences and placed food on her plate. Abigail glanced up to see Titus watching her, a look of appreciation in his eyes.

Eliza cleared her throat. They both looked at her, then went back to their business. "So, Titus," Eliza said, lifting her fork in the air, "tell me more about yourself." The chattering at the table stopped. With a curious glance, Mrs. Matthews looked at Eliza. Titus squirmed in his chair, seemingly uncomfortable with the attention.

"Eliza, we've talked about me many times before. This is Christmas. There is much more to discuss."

"All right, then," she said, not to be deterred, "I can tell you about me."

Heat flamed Abigail's cheeks at Eliza's selfishness.

"You may not know this, but I've actually won awards for my needlepoint. I have quite a lot of things at home decorated with needlepoint—pillows, pillowcases, and the like. But of course, I brought only the bare essentials to work with when I had to come here." Instead of reflecting gratitude for a roof over her head, Eliza's voice was tainted with disgust.

Feeling her Irish blood shift from simmer to a rolling boil, Abigail opened her mouth to say something but caught her mother's discrete shake of the head. Abigail clamped her mouth shut. All the angry words bunched in her throat, and she swallowed them.

It took two hard swallows.

"You do a beautiful job with your needlepoint, Eliza. I

noticed the pillow you are currently working on is very nice, indeed," Mother said.

Eliza straightened her shoulders and lifted her nose, every so slightly, but said nothing.

Mother changed the subject. "You know, I was reading in the newspaper—"

"Did you hear about the woman who tried to befriend a prison inmate?" Eliza interrupted. "It seems while attending to the female prisoner, the kind woman had taken quite ill. The prisoner gave her a drink of water, sprinkled with morphine, which promptly put the volunteer to sleep. When she awoke, she was void of her teeth." Eliza laughed heartily.

"Oh dear," Mother said with a gasp. "That's positively scandalous."

"I'd be in a fix without me teeth, I can tell ye that," Gramma admitted.

Eliza nodded her head. "The prisoner took out the woman's teeth for the gold in them. The police found them later stuffed in her things."

Mother *tsked* and shook her head. "What is the world coming to?"

"I think it's funny," Eliza continued.

" 'Twouldn't be so funny if ye didn't have ye teeth," Gramma chided before chewing heartily on a piece of turkey. Then she shrugged. "I'm afraid they wouldn't get much from me, though, they wouldn't. Not a piece of gold in there. Me teeth be worth their weight in gold to me, though." Gramma laughed at her own joke.

"I still think it's funny," Eliza said, lifting an eyebrow and lifting her nose in a snoot.

Mother pinned Eliza with a look that said *enough.* "I think it's quite unfortunate, Eliza."

"It's Christmas. We should talk about happy things," Abigail put in.

Eliza scowled at her.

"If everyone is quite finished, I say it's time we share our presents," Father said pleasantly, as if trying to lighten the tension in the room.

Abigail's heart squeezed. Her mother had wanted the day to be perfect, and Eliza seemed bent on ruining it. Why did she have to come, anyway? The sooner she could leave, the better. She was just like her father.

Dusk has settled over the town as the group shared their presents and got to know one another. By the time Titus, his family, and Gramma left the gathering, a wintry moon hung suspended above a cluster of oak trees. Making their way out the door, Abigail called out to him. "Oh, Titus, I almost forgot." He turned to her. She ran into the kitchen and back to the door.

Since her family had given Titus a new hat for Christmas, Abigail had decided to bake some cookies for him and his family as her gift. Though it wasn't as nice as the scarf Eliza had given him, she decided she preferred something a little less personal. She lifted a plate of assorted cookies to him. "I know it's just cookies, but I baked them for you and your family." A twinge of embarrassment heated her cheeks.

He stood looking at her without saying a word, but he didn't have to. His eyes spoke of his pleasure.

"What a lovely gesture, Abigail. A gift of time is one of the finest treasures of all," Mrs. Matthews said.

Abigail heard Eliza "humph" behind her, then clomp up the stairs.

Gramma winked at Abigail.

"Well, Merry Christmas," Abigail said. A flurry of holiday greetings filled the room as the Matthews family and Gramma went through the door, allowing the wisp of a wintry breeze to slip inside before they stepped into the cold night.

❧

By the time Titus had dropped off Gramma O'Connor and reached their home, he was pretty worn out from the day. Lifting his sleeping sister from the carriage, he hurried through their front door with Ma close behind. After laying Jenny on her bed, he braced himself for the cold, went back outside, took care of their horse and wagon, then went back in the house. Ma had hot coffee waiting.

Long legs stretched out before him as he settled into his seat. "This is nice, Ma. Thanks," he said, wrapping his cold fingers around the warm cup.

She sat across from him at the table, took a sip of coffee, and looked at him. "We had a wonderful Christmas, didn't we?"

"That we did," he agreed.

"Jenny seemed taken with Abigail."

"I noticed that," he said with pleasure.

"Abigail is a fine young lady."

Titus looked at Ma, throwing her a look that said he knew exactly what she was up to. "There's no denying that."

"She'll make some man a fine wife one day."

"I suppose so," he said matter-of-factly, hiding a smile behind his cup.

"Tell me what you think of Eliza," Ma said, studying his face.

Titus shook his head and blew out a sigh. "Now there's a woman who could make a man choose the company of his horse."

Ma seemed to struggle with holding back a chuckle. "I must agree she is, well, a tad bold." Ma took another drink. "It's obvious she's taken by you."

He whistled. "I know you're a praying woman, Ma, and the man Eliza O'Connor snags will need much prayer, but I don't plan on getting snagged."

"By her?"

"By her."

She looked at him, her eyes twinkling. He suddenly realized he had been trapped. "All right, I see what you're doing here."

Ma feigned innocence.

He rubbed his head. "Aw, Ma, I plan on getting married one day. When I find the right woman."

Her eyebrows lifted.

"What?"

"Anybody I know?"

He smirked at her. "I'll let you know when I meet her. Until then—"

She cut him off. "I'll keep praying."

He smiled, rose from the table, and dropped a kiss on her head. "I love you, Ma," he said before taking his cup to the sink. "Good night."

☙

Titus had made a habit of attending church with the O'Connors but was no closer to finding out anything substantial against the family. It seemed everyone liked them. He could see why.

After lunch, the O'Connors prepared to go visit Gramma, who had felt poorly and stayed home from church. Titus needed to get back home to Ma and Jenny. He started to board his wagon when he realized he'd left his hat on the kitchen table. Remembering the O'Connors left their home unlocked, he decided he'd better retrieve his hat. Barnabas greeted him with a wagging tail when Titus stepped back into the house. Titus stooped and scratched the old hound behind the ears, then walked over to the table where he'd left his hat.

As he turned to go, he walked through the hall and noticed the open door to the sitting room. This was Mr. O'Connor's study area. He glanced in as he walked by and noticed a box by Mr. O'Connor's chair. Though the notion of getting even with this family lessened with each passing day, he couldn't deny he hadn't given up on the idea entirely. No one was home. They need never know. He stood in the doorway, biting his lip, hesitating, wondering.

Before he could think any further, his footsteps carried him into the room. He scrunched down by the box, and though guilt plagued him, he reached for the box and opened it. Assorted business papers filled the pine box, most of which meant nothing to him. Then he saw the letter to his pa from Mr. O'Connor, agreeing to sell his remaining shares of the business to Pa. He quickly scanned the letter, taking in the fact Mr. O'Connor did mention diversifying and making sure Pa wanted full ownership. Titus stared into books that lined the wall, though not really seeing them. By the sounds of the letter, Mr. O'Connor didn't want to sell off the business. The warning to diversify was obvious.

Mr. O'Connor had been telling the truth. He felt as if a load of bricks had been lifted from his shoulders. All this time with all his bitterness and resentment, he had been wrong. Maybe Ma was right. Maybe Mr. O'Connor had not tried to break their family. Pa's wrong choices took them there. Titus's hand shook with thoughts of days wasted, energies spent, bitterness eating away at him.

He heard a jostling at the front door. Barnabas ran to the door and started barking. Quickly, Titus placed the letter back in the appropriate place in the box. Grabbing his hat, he hurried through the sitting-room door and walked down the hallway toward the front door. Eliza stepped in.

"Hush up, you no-account dog!" She looked up and saw Titus. "Oh, my, you startled me," she said, holding a gloved hand to her throat.

"Sorry. I just came in to get my hat," he explained.

She eyed him with suspicion. Her gaze glanced around the area. His pulse raced in his ears. He hoped he had put everything back in order.

"Yes, well, I need a heavier cloak," she said. "Would you mind helping me out of this one?" Before he could answer, she walked over to him and turned around with her back to him. He slipped off her cloak. She turned around, mere inches from his face. "Thank you," she whispered. He could feel her breath on his cheek.

She raised her arms to his chest and with a gloved hand ran her finger down his jaw. "You know, Titus, I'd really like to get to know you better." Her tone was one of definite boldness. He took a step back.

"Titus, why do you avoid me?" A pout played on her lips. "Aren't you attracted to me?" She walked over to him again.

This time her arms went up around his neck. "Don't you desire me even the least little bit?" Pulling his head farther down to her until their lips finally met, she pressed her mouth hard against his own. He wanted to pull away, but he hadn't kissed a woman in such a long time. A warning seemed to sound inside him. He mentally shook himself and broke free, pulling her arms from his neck. He stepped back.

"I've got to go, Eliza."

She lifted her chin. He felt pride rather than modesty stained her cheeks red. The look on her face spelled trouble. He knew that look because he'd worn it himself until ten minutes ago.

Just then the front door opened. They both turned to see Abigail.

She stopped short, as if she realized she had interrupted an awkward moment. "I'm sorry. I didn't mean to intrude."

"No intrusion at all," Titus said, his heart feeling lighter by the minute. Especially with the sight of Abigail. His reassuring smile seemed to put her at ease, though the scorn on Eliza's face must have told her a different story altogether.

He brushed by Abigail and turned back. Seeing Eliza's back to him, he looked at Abigail. "I'll see you tomorrow," he said in hushed tones, his gaze lingering on her.

ten

The next morning, Abigail stepped into the blazing yellow sunlight. The town glistened in a whitewash of snow. The January air smelled clean as a new year. An early chill prickled her skin as Abigail stepped toward the carriage. Stopping short of the carriage seat, Abigail turned to Titus, wondering how to approach the matter.

"I was hoping maybe after we visit Barnabas House, if we might perhaps—well, uh, I was wondering. . ."

Titus appeared perplexed by her struggle with the words.

She took a deep breath. "Could we stop by your house? I have something for Jenny."

He looked like he might object, then seemed to think better of it. His glance went to the cloth rag doll in her hands.

She held it up. "This is Laura. She used to be mine when I was a little girl."

His eyebrows spiked upward. "You can't give her something so valuable, Abigail." His words were soft.

Lifting her head in confidence, she looked at him. "A wise friend once told me that when you love someone, you give them your best gift, just like God did when He gave His Son, Jesus."

Titus stared into her eyes, never blinking. "Well, I guess I can't argue that." He waited a moment, still looking into her eyes. "Thank you, Abigail." His voice was husky and low. His hand touched her arm. He had never touched her, even slightly, unless it was to help her into the carriage. Somehow she felt something was changing between them.

The thrill of presenting her doll to Jenny kept Abigail excited all morning while working at Barnabas House. Once they arrived at the Matthewses' home, Abigail was taken back by the poverty surrounding them. It made her admire Titus all the more. Rather than wallowing in self-pity, he got out there and made the effort to feed his family. The more she thought about him, the more she liked him.

He helped her from the carriage. "I apologize for the area." His hand swept across the neighborhood.

"Please." Abigail stopped his hand midway and held it. "Don't. I didn't come here to see the neighborhood. I came here to see your ma and Jenny."

"You're a wonder, you know that?"

She laughed. "I'll bet that's what you say to all the ladies." Her steps continued toward the door.

He laughed and jumped forward to keep up with her. He grabbed her hand and turned her to him. "No. Just you."

Abigail swallowed hard. The front door opened. "I thought I heard someone." Mrs. Matthews's face sparkled with pleasure. "Abigail, so good to see you. Come in. Come in."

Once inside, Mrs. Matthews pulled Abigail into a warm embrace. When they parted, she smiled and pointed to Jenny. The little girl lay in a heap on a mattress on the floor. She looked up at Abigail, a huge smile on her face, a twinkle in her eyes.

"Well, hello, little one," Abigail said, walking across the floor and stooping down to her. Holding the rag doll behind her back, she said, "I have something for you, Jenny."

The little girl's eyes lit with excitement. With her strong arms, she pushed herself up.

"Funny how they have the strength when they need it," Mrs. Matthews said with a laugh.

Abigail smiled and brought the rag doll in front of her. "This is for you."

Tears made wet tracks down the little girl's cheeks. "Oh," Abigail said with a gasp. She pulled Jenny into a hug. "You like it then?" she asked, once she released her.

Jenny nodded.

"I'm so glad, Jenny. You see, this is Laura. She used to be my doll when I was a little girl." Jenny smiled and immediately pulled the doll tight against her chest.

Abigail stood.

"How about some coffee?" Mrs. Matthews asked them.

Abigail looked to Titus. "Fine with me, if Abigail doesn't mind."

"I'd like that," she said.

"Good."

The three sat down at the kitchen table. Though the place looked old and revealed little wealth, Abigail noticed the room was clean. An apple pie baked in the oven, spreading a pleasant scent around the room.

"You finally made your apple pie," Titus teased.

"I wanted to save it for a special day. And as it turned out, today is special. Jenny received a wonderful gift from Abigail." Mrs. Matthews looked at Jenny and smiled, then turned to Abigail. "Thank you."

"My pleasure. I did have another matter I wanted to talk with you about," Abigail ventured.

Titus looked at her with surprise.

"I wanted to know if I might come over and work with Jenny on her words." Seeing the surprise on their faces, she hurried on. "I'm a certified teacher, you know, and I can get some books. If you'll allow me, maybe I can help her."

"You would do this for our Jenny?" Mrs. Matthews asked with disbelief.

"Of course."

More charity. Titus knew Abigail's heart was right, but he didn't like charity. Even from her. "I don't think so, Abigail," he said.

Abigail and Mrs. Matthews looked to him with a start.

"But why, Titus?" Mrs. Matthews wanted to know.

"We don't need charity. When I save enough money, we'll get the help we need."

"You'll allow your stubborn pride to keep your sister from getting help?" There went her Irish temper again. She took a deep breath.

His jaw set, his cold, hard gaze held hers.

"What do you say, Mrs. Matthews?"

Mrs. Matthews looked from Abigail, to her daughter, to Titus. "I say, I love my son." She caught his attention, then continued. "But this time he is wrong." She turned to Abigail. "I would appreciate anything you can do."

Titus took a deep breath. He drank his coffee more quickly than anyone should drink something hot, then he went outside.

Abigail stood to leave.

"Don't worry. He'll come around. He's got his pa's stubborn pride."

Abigail smiled at the kind woman. "I'll be by three times a week."

"May God bless you for your kindness."

❧

Two weeks later found Titus walking around the O'Connor property, trying to sort things through in his mind. He supposed Abigail's charity caused old doubts to resurface. Though he had found the letter in Mr. O'Connor's box revealing some of the man's intentions, Titus still had suspicions. It didn't strike him right that his pa would bear the entire brunt of things. Why would he put everything into that business? Things didn't add up. Titus and his pa didn't talk much about business things, but Titus thought his pa was a wise businessman. Had Titus been wrong?

With gusto, he kicked a pebble in his path. He was tired of thinking. Abigail had been to their home several times now. Jenny's face lit up every time Abigail walked into the room. He couldn't deny her presence seemed to help Jenny. The way Abigail pored over those books with Jenny, the painstaking lessons for a girl who showed little response, he had to admit were admirable. Still, he didn't like feeling in debt to the O'Connor family just to appease their consciences.

He shouldn't have taken his family to the O'Connors' for Christmas. That's what started the whole mess. And he couldn't understand Eliza. Why was she staying there if she so obviously hated it? Did they have guilt over something done to her, as well? Maybe he should find out just why she was there.

Ma said pray about it. How could he pray when he hadn't talked to God in more than a year? Titus once served Him, but that was before everything went wrong. *You don't serve God because He does things for you, Titus. You serve Him because of who He is.* His ma's words haunted him. Aw, why did she have to pray all the time! He kicked the ground once more with his boot.

A movement in the front of his house caught his attention. Abigail was waving. Upon seeing her, his heart flipped. Why did he do that? He didn't want to turn weak-kneed at the sight of her. But he did.

Every time he saw her.

With a heavy sigh, he walked straight toward the woman who had turned his world upside down.

੩ৡ

On Thursday afternoon, Eliza stayed outside talking to Titus while Abigail visited with Gramma.

"Does it bother you?" Gramma asked.

"What?"

"That your cousin visits with the handsome chauffeur?"

"Why should it?"

"Never be trustin' an answer that asks a question, said me pa." Gramma laughed, causing Abigail to smile.

"All right, maybe a little."

Gramma gave her a knowing look. "Ye care about him. I can see it in ye eyes, wee one." Gramma pointed her crooked finger at Abigail. "He cares about ye, too."

Abigail shook her head.

"You didn't know?"

"No, Gramma, he doesn't. He cares about Eliza."

"Surely ye don't think so? If he does, he's not the man I be thinkin'."

"He spends time with her."

"She spends time with him," Gramma corrected. "There's a difference. Ye must trust ye heart again, Abigail. Ye be afraid to trust. Ye fear getting hurt?"

Abigail nodded. Tears spilled down her cheeks, and she couldn't imagine what had gotten into her.

Gramma stretched her arms wide and walked over to Abigail, pulling her into a hug. " 'Tis no' wrong to fear, Abigail, darling. 'Tis only wrong to let it hold ye prisoner." Gramma lifted Abigail's chin and looked her full in the face. "Life, 'tis full of hurts. Things are not always what they seem, and expectations are set too high. People fail. Remember, we make mistakes, too." Gramma smiled and kissed Abigail's temple. "Never forget, everyone is imperfect. 'Tis why we need a Savior."

Abigail nodded and blew her nose into a handkerchief. "Thank you, Gramma. Pray that I can trust again. I really want to. I just don't know how."

"I will pray."

Just then the door flew open, letting all the winter's chill in and the stove's warmth out. Eliza stood in the doorway. "Are you ready to go yet, Abigail?" she whined, one hand on her hip. "I'm tired."

Abigail looked at Gramma and lifted a weak smile. She stood to her feet and kissed Gramma good-bye. "I'm coming," she called to Eliza, who was already down the stairs, leaving the door wide open. Abigail ran to the door and pulled it almost closed. "Thanks for everything, Gramma. I love you."

"I love ye, Abigail darling."

Abigail turned to go, wondering about the glimpse of pain that flickered across Gramma's face.

❧

Later that evening, sunken between soft sheets and plump blankets and pillows, Abigail felt she was lying on a cloud. She did some of her best thinking in the comfort of her bed. Barnabas whined until she stroked his fur. Then with a look of satisfaction, the mutt trotted clumsily to the foot of the bed.

Watching him, Abigail laughed. She leaned back once more and stared at the ceiling. Since her visit with Gramma, she had felt uneasy. She wasn't sure why. Maybe it was the realization of knowing that her feelings for Titus were growing, or maybe it was the shadow on Gramma's face when Abigail left. What was that about? Did she think Abigail wouldn't trust another man? Did she fear Abigail's heart would break again? If so, why?

She wanted to pray yet struggled. Her thoughts toward Eliza hadn't been exactly Christian. How could God hear Abigail when her heart had shadows where Eliza was concerned? She didn't like herself when she acted that way. It just seemed Eliza brought out the worst in her. She shook her head. No, she couldn't blame someone else for her own actions. It was time to change things. This seemed as good a time as any.

Abigail slipped from her covers and knelt beside her bed, asking the Lord for forgiveness for her treatment of Eliza. After all, the Lord loved Abigail enough to die for her, and she didn't deserve it. In her own strength, Abigail had to admit she didn't have it in her to love Eliza. It would take God's strength to work through her and make it happen. Amid a flurry of tears, Abigail laid her heart's cry at the foot of God's throne, knowing when she had risen, that the Savior had heard and answered her prayer.

She blew out the light in her lantern, then slipped beneath her covers once again. Tomorrow would be a good day. No matter the circumstances.

❧

Abigail slept the night through like a baby. By the time the morning's light had flooded into her room, she felt refreshed and fully alive. She could hardly wait to start her day. God had worked in her heart; now came the time to roll up her sleeves and get to work.

Quickly, she dressed and pulled her hair back with a ribbon, allowing the curls to flow down her back. She took one glance at the looking glass and decided her appearance would do for breakfast.

Practically running down the stairs, with Barnabas right on her heels, she had a definite hop to her walk by the time she made it into the kitchen.

"Well, someone is feeling mighty chipper this morning," Mother said with a smile.

"I feel wonderful today," Abigail replied.

"Well, I'm glad someone does," Eliza said as she entered. "Is the coffee ready?" She lifted sleepy eyes toward the stove.

Mother laughed. "It's ready. You ladies go sit at the table, and I'll bring you your breakfast."

"Can I help?" Abigail asked.

"No, dear, I can manage."

As she walked to the table, carrying the coffee pot, Mother explained that Father had to meet his boss at the railroad station early that morning. "What's on your schedule today, Abigail?" she asked, pouring coffee into the empty cups.

"Barnabas House has taken on more workers, so I'm not needed as often. I miss the kids, but Jenny helps fill the void. I thought I'd go over and work with her today."

Mother smiled, placing the coffeepot back on the stove. She sat down once more. "How about you, Eliza? What are your plans?"

Eliza let out a long sigh and glared at Mother. "Same thing day after day. Work on my needlepoint, take a walk, wait, wait, wait on word from my pa."

Tempted to snap a retort to the young woman for her ingratitude, Abigail felt a prick of conscience and threw up a silent prayer for help. This whole business was going to be harder than she thought.

"You can go with me today, Eliza, if you'd like."

She looked at Abigail. "Well, I wouldn't like. I don't want to sit around while you're teaching a girl who won't even talk. I don't know why you waste your time."

A spurt of anger shot through Abigail in an instant. Her

body trembled, but she said nothing. Yes, this assignment was much harder than she had anticipated.

Mother winked at Abigail.

Just then, a knock sounded at the door. Barnabas bounded to the door ahead of Mother. Abigail could hear Titus's voice from the hallway. In a moment, boots scuffled against the floor, and Titus entered the kitchen. "I'll get your coffee, Titus."

He looked up rather sheepishly at Abigail. "Morning, Abigail." Almost as an afterthought, he turned to Eliza. "Eliza," he said with a tip of his head. She suddenly sprang to life. Her back was straighter, fingers absently brushed stray hairs into place, and a smile found its way to her face.

Mother poured some coffee and handed the cup to Titus, who stood at the entrance. "Come in and join us."

He stretched out at the table near Abigail. Eliza frowned. Mother attempted to sit, then seemed to think better of it. "Oh!" she said with a start. "I almost forgot. I stopped and picked up the mail in town yesterday, Abigail. You have a letter."

Abigail was surprised. She couldn't imagine who would have written to her.

Mother walked over to the counter, then walked back to Abigail with a reserved smile, holding an envelope. She paused, then handed it to her daughter.

Abigail took it, wondering why the hesitation. She glanced down at the envelope and saw the return address.

It simply read "Jonathan Clark."

eleven

Abigail glanced up to see Titus staring at her with a question in his eyes. Eliza seemed to sense something going on and perked up considerably.

"So, who is Jonathan?" she asked Abigail, though her gaze stayed firmly fixed on Titus.

Mother piped up, "He's an old friend of Abigail's."

Abigail shot her a grateful look, then stared into her breakfast plate. She didn't want to talk about anything just now. Suddenly, she didn't want breakfast.

"Dear, if you'd like to go read your letter, that's fine."

Abigail nodded and made her way from the room. "Well, he must have been a special friend," she heard Eliza say with a laugh. The scooting of a chair sounded from the kitchen. Abigail slipped into the sitting room and heard heavy footsteps in the hallway and finally the opening of the front door. She glanced out the window to see Titus walking across the lawn, a scowl on his face. She wondered if Eliza had said something more to upset him.

Turning her attention back to the letter, Abigail settled into a chair and began to open the white envelope. She read through the words that told her his job was going well and he was glad to be back east. But the next few lines took her breath. "I miss you. I thought I could get along, but it's hard being here without you. I see you everywhere I turn."

The letter continued with more superficial news, and her eyes kept going back to the part about him missing her. She read it over and over. Finally, she leaned back in the chair. What did this mean? Would he come back to Chicago? Did she want him to? She wasn't sure anymore.

Her thoughts flitted to Titus. Every day her feelings grew a little stronger toward him. She wondered if he sensed it at all. He seemed to enjoy her company, though she didn't know if he wanted only friendship or something more between them.

Eliza knocked at the door. Abigail motioned her in.

"Good news?" Eliza asked, looking hopeful.

"It was a nice letter."

Eliza plopped at the desk chair. "Tell me about him."

Abigail didn't want to share intimate details with Eliza. They did not have that kind of friendship. In fact, Abigail felt a twinge of resentment toward Eliza for asking. After all, it was quite obvious she wanted to glean information for her own selfish purposes. To win Titus.

Maybe that's what troubled Abigail about Eliza. Abigail was jealous. The thought irritated her even more. Why should she be jealous? It wasn't as though Abigail and Titus had a relationship of any kind. He could certainly see whom he wished. She would not fight with Eliza over him as if they were silly schoolgirls.

Abigail rose to her feet. "There's not much to tell, really. He's a good friend." With that, she left the room, leaving Eliza alone with her schemes.

"Mother, I think I'll go visit Sophia. Would you like me to pick up anything for you while I'm out?"

Her mother appeared at the drawing-room door. "No, dear, I don't need anything." She glanced curiously at Abigail. "Everything all right?"

"It's fine," Abigail said with a smile.

Mother nodded, wiping her hands on a towel.

"I'll just let Titus know." Abigail grabbed her cloak and went outside with Barnabas trotting at her heels, his head up, ears pricked with the thrill of an adventure, and a long wagging tail that spiraled into a gentle curl at the very tip. Abigail looked at him and laughed.

She glanced around at the spots of persistent grass that poked through the melting snow. The sun breathed down warm rays, causing the remaining snow to sparkle and glitter upon the lawn.

Abigail took in a huge helping of new morning air. "Isn't this wonderful, Barnabas?" She looked at her faithful companion, who looked up at her in a satisfied fashion, as though he couldn't agree more. Bending over, she scratched his head. "You're always so agreeable, not like some people," she said with a glance across her shoulder toward the house.

"And who might that be?" Titus's strong voice startled her. She jerked back to look at him.

"Oh, I—"

Something in his expression made her heart go soft. When did he start affecting her in this way? He smiled. "Were you looking for me?"

She threw a thankful grin. "Yes. I wanted to know if you could take me to Sophia's in, say, half an hour?"

"Be happy to." He hunkered down and scratched Barnabas. "How you doing, ole boy?"

Abigail watched the scene and smiled. Barnabas had grown very fond of Titus. The dog happily nuzzled into Titus, leaning into the scratches as if he were having the most pleasurable of experiences.

"I do believe if he were a cat, he'd purr," Titus said with a laugh.

Abigail laughed, too.

Titus finally stood and looked at Abigail again. He lingered a moment. "You doing all right?"

His question warmed her. The fact that he cared meant a lot to her. She nodded.

"Don't let anyone hurt you."

The comment caught her off guard. Before she could respond, he continued. "He did hurt you once, didn't he?"

"How did you know?"

"Your expression tells a lot."

She looked at the ground.

"Do you still care about him?"

His bold question surprised her. Eliza must have been rubbing off on him. She nodded. "But not in the way I did before."

He shoved his right hand into his pocket. "That's good news."

Her head jerked up with a start. "It is?"

"Yes, Abigail. It is." His face broke into a happy grin. Their gazes locked, and they stood, lost in the wonder of the moment, neither saying a word.

"I'll get the carriage," he finally said.

Abigail smiled and practically floated back to the house, carried on the whisper of the wind.

❧

"Look at you," Abigail said when she entered the Thread Bearer and saw Sophia stand and come toward her. "You are a beautiful mother-to-be." They embraced, a glow emanating from Sophia's face.

"Thank you." She grabbed Abigail's hand and led her into the kitchen. Promptly she pointed to a chair at the table where Abigail could sit while Sophia started the kettle for tea. "So, tell me what brings you here today." Sophia settled onto her seat and smiled at her friend.

Abigail proceeded to tell her about the letter from Jonathan and finally her exchange with Titus before she left to come to Sophia's shop.

"What do you think of it all, Abigail?"

"I don't know what to think."

"Well, there's no question of Titus's interests. He's made that quite clear," she said with a smile. The water boiled, and Sophia got up and prepared their tea and poured it into thick mugs. She placed them on the table.

"How do you feel about Jonathan?"

Abigail toyed with a curl at the side of her face. "That's just it. I don't know anymore."

"It's different now, though, isn't it?"

Abigail nodded. "Do you think I ever really loved him?"

Sophia shrugged. "It's hard for me to say. Only you can really answer that, but I'm thinking no. Another person could not take his place so soon."

"You mean Titus?"

Sophia nodded. "He has, you know."

Abigail stared into her cup. "Yes, I know."

"Is that a bad thing?"

Abigail looked up. "I don't know. I mean, I know he cares about me, but it seems like something is holding him back. I just don't know what it is."

"Maybe he's afraid you won't feel the same way. Does he know about Jonathan?"

"A little." Abigail looked toward the distant wall. "I suppose he could be afraid of my feelings for Jonathan. Although, I think I may have cleared that matter up for him in our conversation before we arrived here."

Sophia grinned. "Perhaps now things will get interesting." She shot an ornery glance at Abigail and they both laughed.

"Are you going to write Jonathan back?"

Abigail thought a moment. "I suppose I will. After all, he will always be my friend."

Sophia nodded. "How are things going with Eliza?"

Inhaling a big breath and blowing it out, Abigail said, "Where do I begin?" She related Eliza's antics and how the Lord was helping Abigail to work through the situation and try to be a friend to her cousin. After some discussion, the two women prayed together; then it was time for Abigail to go.

"I'll see you soon, Sophia. You know, I can't wait to spoil your baby," Abigail said with a laugh.

"That makes three of us!" Sophia replied before shifting into her seat at the sewing machine. The hum of the machine started once again as Abigail slipped through the door.

❧

Not much later, Titus took Abigail to Barnabas House. She walked over to her station to check on the children's progress with their studies. Julie Barnes, the woman who in recent days had volunteered to share responsibilities with Abigail, stood smiling.

"Miss Abigail!" Katie O'Grady shot out of her chair and squeezed her arms tight around Abigail's skirts.

"Hello, Katie!" Abigail bent down and hugged the little girl. Soon the other children followed suit and gathered around Abigail.

"We've missed you," said a brown-haired boy with freckles sprinkled across his nose. The others nodded in agreement.

"And I've missed you." She took time to hug each one. She glanced up at Julie. "I'm sorry to disrupt, Julie."

Julie smiled. "No problem at all. They've been asking for you. I'm glad you came in."

Soon the children were back in their seats, busily at work. Abigail checked on their progress with Julie and found they were doing just fine. Truth be known, Abigail missed serving as she once had at Barnabas House, but Julie's help freed Abigail to work more with Jenny Matthews.

Once satisfied the children were in good hands, Abigail walked through the room to leave. Mary O'Grady stopped her.

"Mary, how are you doing? It's so good to see you!"

Mary pulled her aside. The largest of smiles spread across her face. She took a deep breath.

Puzzled, Abigail looked at her. "Mary, what is it?"

"Christopher asked me to marry him."

"What?" Abigail said with a squeal. "That's wonderful, Mary!" She pulled her into an enormous hug. "I'm so happy for you both. When is the big day?"

"We're getting married Saturday, February 1, here at Barnabas House." Mary's eyes sparkled with excitement. "We're inviting the workers and the people who come in here most often. Just a little neighborhood gathering."

"Oh, Mary, how wonderful for you and Katie!" Another hug. "Let me know if I can help in any way."

"Please tell your chauffeur, too. He and Christopher have become good friends."

"Really? I didn't know that."

Mary nodded. "He slips out for coffee with him while you're here."

Abigail laughed. "All right, I'll see that he knows."

When she stepped out of Barnabas House, her heart was light with the good news and the thought that love could strike anyone at any moment. Life was good.

"Hello, you ready to go?" Titus reached a hand to her as her foot landed on the last step.

Her heart flipped as she nodded to him. Yes, life was good.

&

Titus took Abigail for her visit with Jenny. When Abigail stepped into the house, she saw Jenny on the floor, clutching Laura, her rag doll, next to her. Jenny glanced up and smiled. She lifted Laura for Abigail to see.

"Oh, I see you're keeping Laura great company," Abigail said upon entering. She turned to Mrs. Matthews. "Hello."

Mrs. Matthews walked over and gave Abigail a hug. "How are you?"

"Fine, thank you. I want to see how my little friend is doing." She walked on over to Jenny.

"I'll get you some hot tea," Mrs. Matthews called.

"Thank you." Abigail hunched down to Jenny, who had pulled herself to an upright position, still holding Laura. She grinned and held Laura out again. Just then Abigail noticed one of Laura's shoes was missing. "Uh-oh, I think her shoe must be in your bed," Abigail said, glancing around.

Jenny stopped smiling and looked down like something was wrong.

"I'm afraid it's not there. We've looked everywhere for her shoe." Mrs. Matthews stood beside her, wringing her hands together.

Abigail frowned. "Hmm, maybe I dropped it at home and just didn't notice. If not, I've seen some shoes for rag dolls at the mercantile. I can take Laura into the store and find one that matches her clothes," Abigail said brightly.

Mrs. Matthews smiled and shook her head. "You're too good to us, Abigail."

&

Titus watched the whole exchange between Abigail, his mother, and sister. As if truth had finally settled over him, he knew that Abigail didn't befriend them out of guilt. She did so out of love. She loved them, and they all loved her. Including Titus. He stepped outside a moment to leave Abigail to teach Jenny. When he had fallen in love with her, he didn't know. He only knew that it had happened. Whether he wanted it to happen or not, the fact remained. He loved Abigail O'Connor. Now what could he do? He couldn't bring this family down after all the kindness they had shown his family, not to mention his love for Abigail.

He took off his hat and scratched his head. Yet he couldn't deny that a tiny part of him still felt uneasy, like a hungry wolf in search of food. He knew, too, if he didn't let it go, the ultimate result would lead to sorrow. He wanted to release it so he could be free to love Abigail. Yet, could he? The wall of bitterness he had built against the O'Connor family was bigger than anything he could break down on his own.

It would take an act of God.

He stepped back into the house and spotted Abigail rising to her feet after she dropped a kiss on Jenny's head.

"I need to take Laura with me and buy her shoes. I'll bring her back." Abigail lifted Laura from Jenny's strong hold. "It's all right, Jenny. I'll bring her back."

Abigail walked over to the door beside Titus and said good-bye to Mrs. Matthews. Titus opened the door, and they prepared to leave when Jenny's voice cracked through the room, stopping them cold.

"Laura!" she wailed.

twelve

Abigail, Titus, and Mrs. Matthews turned to Jenny with a start. Jenny's arms were stretched out toward her doll, tears streaming down her face. Mrs. Matthews ran to her. She fell at her daughter's feet. "Jenny, you talked!" Tears flooding her own cheeks, Mrs. Matthews grabbed Jenny hard against her and rocked back and forth.

Abigail and Titus exchanged a glance of disbelief. She walked over to return the doll but stood aside a respectable distance to give Mrs. Matthews a moment with her daughter. When they finally parted, Abigail returned Laura. "I'll find shoes for her without taking her," Abigail said as she gently placed Laura back into the sobbing child's arms.

Jenny's tears slowed to a trickle as she held her doll close, patting her back, rocking back and forth. An occasional hiccup escaped her. Abigail leaned down. "I'm sorry, Jenny. I didn't mean to hurt you. I won't take Laura from you."

Jenny looked at Abigail. Her wide eyes pooled with tears, and her chin quivered slightly. "Laura," she said simply.

Abigail ran her hand along Jenny's soft, blond hair and nodded. "Laura."

Titus waited close by. Standing to her feet, Abigail stepped out of the way so Titus could get near his sister. He immediately crouched down beside Jenny and began to smooth her hair away from her face. The tenderness in his eyes, the gentle touches made Abigail's heart squeeze. The love he displayed for his family moved her more than anything. He would make a wonderful father someday. That thought made her blush. Seeing such affection coming from him for his sister made Abigail uncomfortable to be a witness. She felt the sight almost too sacred for her presence.

Her footsteps whispered across the wooden planks to the front door. She turned once more and looked at the family, then snuggled into her winter wraps and stepped into the open air.

Huddled against a corner of the porch, she waited for Titus to come out. In a few minutes, he joined her. "You didn't need to come out here."

"I wanted to give your family time together. It was a special moment."

Titus walked over to her, pulled her gloved hands into his, and looked into her face. "You are special, Abigail. And I thank you for what you're doing for Jenny."

She felt herself blush under his gaze. He didn't blink as he continued to stare into her eyes. Almost in slow motion, his head bent forward, and he pressed her waiting lips with his own. The tender kiss, moist and sweet as the morning dew, lasted a heartbeat, but Abigail knew she would remember it for days to come.

❧

By the time Abigail and Titus returned home that evening, her heart felt light as a feather. He helped her out of the carriage, his hand holding on to hers longer than necessary. "I had a wonderful day, Abigail."

She swallowed hard. "Me, too, Titus."

"I'll see you in the morning," he said, his voice low and soft. He released her hand, tipped his hat, and turned to put the carriage away.

Abigail watched him a moment, wondering how she could feel this way toward him when she thought she had been in love with Jonathan. The thought frightened her a little. What if she wasn't really in love? She had been fooled once. Yet something told her this was definitely different. An icy breeze whipped through her cloak, breaking her free from her musings. She pulled the wool closer to her neck and headed for her house. It had been a wonderful day.

When she stepped into the house, a flurry of barks

assailed her as did Barnabas's paws as he jumped and pushed against her. He wouldn't quiet down until she took the time to say hello. With affection, she rubbed him a moment, then she stood and shook the snow from her outer wraps and pulled off her boots. Placing her cloak on a nearby peg, she walked into the drawing room to find Eliza sitting in front of a blazing fire in the stone fireplace, studying the stitches on the cloth in her hand. The room smelled of pine logs and spiced cider. Abigail took a deep breath, thinking the scent heavenly.

Eliza looked up with a scowl. "Where have you been?"

The anger in Eliza's voice took Abigail by surprise. "I went to see Sophia, Barnabas House, and then over to see Jenny Matthews."

Eliza's eyes tightened to slits. "Well, how convenient."

"What do you mean?"

"Little Miss Charity Worker out spreading cheer to all around her. Of course, if her kindness happens to spill upon the sister of one handsome chauffeur, all the better," Eliza said, her voice thick with jealousy.

Abigail did not want to play into her hand. She prayed a quick prayer to get through the anger Eliza's words had evoked. Taking a deep breath, Abigail walked over to her cousin. "Look, Eliza, I don't want to fight with you. You're my cousin and I want—"

"You want," Eliza spat. "What about what I want? No one cares one whit what I want!"

Abigail suddenly knew this was about more than mere jealousy. This was about Uncle Edward dropping his daughter off in their care. It was about Eliza feeling sorry for herself.

Filled with compassion for her cousin, Abigail measured her words carefully. "I know things haven't been easy for you coming here."

"Easy? I'll say it's not been easy! How would you like to be ripped from your home and stay with people whom you hardly know? And then Titus comes along, giving me hope of rescue from my eternal boredom, but he takes no interest in me whatsoever. Of course you've seen to that!" Eliza glared at Abigail as though she could chew her up and spit her out.

Abigail stared at her, not knowing what to say.

"You are in love with him, aren't you?" Eliza said in a sneering voice.

When Abigail said nothing, Eliza stabbed the needle into her cloth piece. "Oh, how nice for the both of you. Abigail, who always gets what she wants, has won once again." Eliza folded her cloth and stood now, inches from Abigail's face. "Just don't turn your back, Abigail. You never know what a woman scorned might do."

Abigail drew in a sharp breath at the comment and stood trembling as she watched her cousin stomp across the room with resentment and anger guiding every step.

❧

A full moon sailed high above him as Titus made his way to the barn. It had been a long week, and he was glad it was Saturday. He was tired and ready to go home. Hearing the snap of a twig behind him, he turned around to see Eliza standing just inside the barn.

"Eliza, what are you doing here?"

Absently running her gloved hand along the doorframe, she pouted, "Can't I come and say hello?"

"I just spent dinner with you," he said, scratching his head.

"Yeah, me and the whole O'Connor family," she said, watching him closely.

What was she up to? Eliza always had something up her sleeve. After she kissed him that night, he'd stayed clear of her. Not one to beat around the bush, he stepped over to her. "What's going on, really, Eliza? Why did you come out here tonight?"

She looked up at him with an innocent look. "Don't you know?"

He shook his head.

"I can't seem to get you to myself for a moment." She lifted her arms around his neck.

"Not this time, Eliza," he said, pulling her arms away from him.

An icy glaze filled her eyes. "Why, because of Abigail?" she spat.

"Listen, I don't know what your game is, but I don't want any part of it," he said, turning toward his wagon.

"Look who's talking. As if you don't have a game!"

He stopped in his tracks and turned to her.

She gave a hollow laugh and lifted her chin. "That's right. I know you're up to something. After catching you lingering outside the study that night, I decided to investigate and see if anything was amiss. So after the family went to bed, I came down and looked around."

His heart thundered against his chest.

"I noticed a tiny edge of paper hanging outside of Uncle Thomas's box by his chair. I opened the box and there was a letter to your father from Uncle. I figured there must have been a reason you wanted to see that." She watched him closely, as if looking for any clues he might give her.

"Now, I may not have all the pieces together in the puzzle yet, but don't play innocent with me. I know I'm not the only one around here with a plan."

"It's not like that, Eliza. At least, not anymore."

She stepped closer. "The way I see it, you need me, and I need you. We can work together and both get what we want." Her eyes flickered with excitement.

"I don't want to bring them down, Eliza." He couldn't believe he was saying that.

She ran a finger along his jawline. "Well, if you change your mind, I'm here," she said in a seductive voice that made him sick. A laugh escaped her before she walked out the door. Fear gripped his heart. Eliza was the type of woman who would do anything to get her way.

Just when he felt things were turning around in his heart, the freedom that had lifted him from bitterness seemed to drain from his soul like life ebbing from a dying man.

Once again he felt trapped, but this time by the bitterness of another.

꙳

Sunday morning Titus once again sat on the church bench with the O'Connor family. Sandwiched between Abigail and Eliza, he felt a bit awkward. Eliza had been following him around like a hovering shadow. He didn't like it at all.

The pastor spoke of Solomon and how he had served the Lord faithfully, then ultimately allowed other gods to infiltrate his heart. Titus wondered how someone could be that strong in their walk, then so blatantly turn from the truth. Then he thought of his own life. Isn't that exactly what he had done? He had once believed. But that was before his father's business was destroyed and the family funds had dwindled, taking Titus's dreams with them.

Even so, he wasn't sure he was ready to change that. A root of bitterness lingered, but God was dealing with him. Of that, he was sure.

By the sermon's end, Titus felt at war with himself. He wanted to get things straightened out with God. The O'Connors seemed to have proven themselves genuine, but he couldn't shake the notion that someone needed to pay for his suffering.

Someone did pay. Jesus.

He pushed the thought aside, not wanting to think about it. Despite his efforts to ignore the matter, though, he could feel his mood diving south. He needed to get home. Think things through.

After the final prayer, the people shuffled across the wooden floor toward the exit. As people crowded in around them, he reached over and touched Abigail's elbow. Seeming to sense it was he, she turned up and smiled. They had just stepped into the sunshine when a voice called from the side. "Abigail!"

Titus and Abigail both turned their heads to see a tall man

with spectacles and a wide smile coming their way, hand extended.

"Jonathan," Abigail said with a smile. Though she hesitated just a moment, she offered her hand in greeting. She turned to Titus and introduced him to Jonathan. Did her face light up with the presence of her old friend, or was Titus imagining it? He felt like a jealous schoolboy. He glanced at Eliza. She tossed him a smirk. Perhaps she could see it, too.

Abigail's preoccupation with her visitor coupled with his own jealousy made Titus sick of heart. Deciding to go home, Titus slipped from the gathering and headed for his wagon.

"Titus," Eliza called out.

He turned to her.

She stepped up to him and raised her hand to his arm. "Just remember what I told you. I'm here for you if you change your mind."

Titus glared at her, then turned back to his wagon. Her laughter taunted him the entire ride home.

thirteen

Abigail took a moment to collect herself from all the excitement Jonathan's visit brought. She and her family stood talking with him in front of the church. Buggies were pulling out and most likely heading home.

While her father talked to Jonathan of business things, Abigail glanced around. She saw Eliza standing with Titus, her hand on his arm. He didn't pull away. Eliza still pursued him; that much was obvious. How did he feel about her? Was she winning him over? Did the kiss Abigail and Titus had shared mean anything to him? She glanced at Jonathan, then back to Titus. Her heart felt a tangle of confusion.

Titus turned and climbed into his wagon without saying good-bye to any of them. Eliza walked over and stood under an apple tree in the distance. She pulled open a book.

Abigail sighed, wondering where her heart would take her, what her future would hold. From a low branch of a nearby tree, a sparrow fluffed his feathers and seemed to snuggle into them. Abigail was reminded of God's love even for the sparrow. If He could take care of the sparrow, He could take care of her. Just then a brown squirrel with a plume of a tail scurried up the tree, startling the sparrow and causing him to fly away, taking Abigail's gaze upward. A spattering of heavy clouds hung low in the wintry sky with occasional patches of soft blue blinking in and out between them.

Abigail thought the day would bring snow. Jonathan loved to ice-skate. Perhaps they could go ice-skating while he was in town. She wondered what had caused Jonathan to return to Chicago and how long he would stay.

"Jonathan, you must join us for lunch," Mother was saying.

Jonathan glanced at Abigail. She smiled at him.

His face broke into the familiar grin that had flipped her heart so many times before. She couldn't deny it felt good to see Jonathan again. Yet things were different somehow. This time, her heart didn't flip. Perhaps she had built a wall to protect herself from further hurt. Not that it mattered; he probably popped in to see her like any good friend would while in town for a visit.

She felt tired and confused. Titus had been acting strange lately, and now with Jonathan showing up, Abigail didn't know what to think about anything.

By the time they got home and ate lunch, midafternoon was upon them. Father glanced out the window, then turned to Abigail and Jonathan. "I know it's cold out there, but with the snowflakes falling, it looks like a good afternoon for a sleigh ride. You're welcome to use our sleigh, Jonathan." A wide grin stretched across his face.

Jonathan turned and smiled at Abigail, his eyes lit with adventure. "What do you say?"

Abigail giggled. "I think it would be fun." Then almost as an afterthought, she looked at Eliza. "Would you like to come along?"

"No, thank you, I'd prefer the company of my needlepoint," she said with a tone that made no apologies for her comment.

Abigail ignored the comment and turned to Jonathan. "I'll grab my things from upstairs. I'll only be a minute."

He nodded.

Before long, they were settled comfortably in the sleigh, the horses hitched and ready to go. She snuggled into the warm skins and breathed deeply of winter's scent. He looked over at her and smiled. "I've missed you."

His comment surprised her. "I've missed you, too," she said. And she meant it.

The horses' *clip-clop* echoed through the afternoon air. Jonathan told her of his new job and new life. Finally, when they had traveled just outside of town, he pulled over near a rotted-out tree. The horses stood pawing the ground, puffs of warm air blowing from their nostrils.

"I've been wrong," Jonathan said, clutching Abigail's hands. "I thought I could go on with my life, that this job was the best thing, and we both should start over, but I was wrong. The vision of you follows me every moment of every day and haunts my dreams at night."

Abigail stared at him, not knowing what to say.

"I love you, Abigail O'Connor." He touched the edge of her hat, pushing it slightly from her face, and he leaned in, his mouth brushing against hers in the familiar way of the past. She kissed him back, surrendering to his touch, relaxing in his arms, until she realized the man she kissed was not Jonathan.

It was Titus.

She pulled away. Her mind and heart became a flurry of confusion and contradictions. First Jonathan loved her, then he didn't. Then Titus cared; now he hovered in secret corners with Eliza. Why did they toy with her heart? She wanted to get away from both of them. Her heart weighed heavy with distrust of everyone. She was tired of being tossed about. Didn't anyone care how she felt? Oh, now she was acting like Eliza. Tears sprang to her eyes.

"Are you all right?"

"I want to go home, Jonathan."

Surprise touched to his face. "Look, Abigail, I'm here for two weeks, and that's it. I have a lot to say to you—"

Abigail turned to him. "I need some time, Jonathan. I don't know what to think about anything right now."

"Does this have anything to do with your chauffeur?"

Abigail wasn't sure how to answer that, because she didn't know the answer. She shook her head. "It has to do with me. I don't want to get hurt anymore." Her words choked to a mere whisper.

He grabbed her by the shoulders until she looked at him again. "I don't want to hurt you. You've got to believe me. I thought I was doing the right thing by both of us when I left. Now I see I was wrong." When she looked at him, he winced.

"But by the look in your eyes, I'm afraid I'm too late."

Jonathan turned around and tugged the horses back into a steady trot. "Give me the week. That's all I ask."

Abigail nodded and leaned into her blankets, wondering what the week would hold.

❧

"Titus, sit down and talk to me. What is troubling you, Son?" Ma asked him as he paced the small room.

His fingers raked through his hair, and he sat in the kitchen chair at the battered wooden table. Ma placed some coffee in front of him. His gaze lingered in his cup. "I don't know."

Ma wisely kept silent and waited.

He looked up. "I think I'm in love with Abigail."

"And that's not a good thing?" she asked with motherly gentleness.

He looked away and fell silent a moment.

Ma seemed to catch on. "She has someone else in her life?" She took a drink of coffee.

His eyes darted back to Ma. "That's just it. I don't know." He blew out a frustrated sigh. "This man Jonathan Clark moved out east, though she had loved him. Now he's back."

Ma put down her cup. "Ah, I see." She paused. "Titus, if she loves you, love will win out."

"And if she doesn't?"

"If she doesn't, then God has other plans."

"God," he spewed. "It's always you and God." He stood to his feet and began pacing again. "What about *my* plans and what *I* want?"

"Your plans, Titus Matthews, will get you into trouble. You must trust the Lord."

"Trust. That's another thing. Abigail would never love me if she knew—" He stopped himself short.

Ma's eyes seared through him. "Titus, what have you done?"

He dropped back into the chair. "I haven't actually done anything, but, well. . ." He looked at Ma. "Well, I wanted to get even with the O'Connors."

"Oh, Titus, no, tell me you haven't hurt this precious family." Ma's eyes pleaded with him.

"I haven't done anything. It's just that Eliza knows I happened upon a paper—"

"Happened upon? Don't color the truth for me, Titus Matthews. Tell me exactly what happened."

He explained the situation with the letter to Pa and how that letter changed his heart. Then about Eliza catching on and knowing he had been searching for something. "So you see, if Eliza puts her spin on things to Abigail, how will I get Abigail to believe that I wasn't using her to get to the truth— or that though it may have started out that way, things changed for me?"

Ma took a drink of coffee and frowned. "Eliza O'Connor needs a good prayer session."

Titus smiled in spite of himself. Those were about the meanest words he could imagine his ma ever saying.

"I see your dilemma, Titus. You'd better pray yourself and ask the Lord to help you through this mess you have made— after you ask Him to clean up your heart."

Titus looked at her a moment. "You pray, Ma. I'm not sure I'm ready."

❦

Monday morning Abigail and Eliza settled into conversation with Gramma at her home once again. Though she added occasional laughter and a comment here and there, Abigail could tell Eliza was not truly concentrating. She kept looking around the room as if searching for something. Abigail couldn't imagine what.

"Have you heard from your father yet, Eliza?"

Eliza shook her head. "Guess they've forgotten about me." She said the words, then stood to her feet and began to meander about the room. Abigail wondered if Eliza was afraid her emotions might show.

"Do you have any books, Gramma?"

Gramma nodded. "There be some in me bedroom. Feel free to look, Eliza. I believe I have a copy of *Little Women*, if ye have never read that one."

Eliza's expression showed surprise. "You've read that, Gramma? I didn't picture you as one to read."

"Ah, I love to read. Just can't see as well as I used to. 'Tis a good book, that one."

Eliza nodded. "I'd like to read it."

Gramma smiled and nodded, pointing toward her room.

Eliza slipped out of the room and into Gramma's room. Abigail and Gramma continued in conversation. Abigail explained her dilemma with Jonathan and Titus.

"I see. If ye thought ye could trust them both fully, Abigail darling, and they both truly loved ye, who would ye choose?"

Abigail bit her lip and twirled a ringlet between her fingers at the side of her face. "I—I don't know for sure. I mean, a few months ago, I was convinced I was in love with Jonathan. Then a few weeks ago, my heart moved to Titus. Now? Well, I just don't know." She looked at Gramma in desperation. "What shall I do?"

"Pray, wee one," Gramma said, reaching over with her old, bent hand and patting Abigail's shoulder.

Abigail nodded. "Sometimes I wish the Lord's answers would come more quickly."

Gramma laughed. "His ways would not be our ways. 'Tis on a different time schedule, He is."

Abigail had to laugh at the thought. She knew Gramma was right. People tried to shape God into their own understanding of Him. He was so much more. Though she still did not have any answers, Abigail felt better just talking about things. She also was certain God would guide her.

"I guess Eliza decided to read in your room," Abigail whispered, leaning into Gramma.

"She tires of me company." Gramma covered a chuckle. "Ye be coming back later this week and letting me know about ye gentlemen friends?" She winked.

Abigail took in a breath. "Gramma, please! You make me sound like a frivolous woman!" They both laughed. "Of course I will be back. I wouldn't miss my visits with you," Abigail said, giving Gramma's hand a squeeze.

"How things be at Barnabas House?"

"Going well. The director is getting married on Saturday. I'm looking forward to going to the wedding. I told you about Mary O'Grady and her daughter, Katie?"

"She'd be the one whose husband left her and later was killed?"

Abigail nodded. "That's who Christopher is marrying. They will make a lovely family. I'm so happy for them all."

"See how God, He works through life's difficulties? No doubt she had many dark hours after her husband left."

"You're right, Gramma."

"God will get us through the questions of life, He will. We need only trust and wait."

Abigail thought a moment and smiled. "How did you get so smart?"

Gramma laughed. "Ah! I'm old. I've seen many things, I have, and listened well."

"Guess I'll have to work on that listening part," Abigail said with a chuckle before rising to her feet. "Well, I really need to go. I'd better get Eliza." She walked to Gramma's bedroom. Peering into the room, Abigail saw Eliza sitting on a rocking chair, looking through what appeared to be a journal of some type. "Ah, you've found something, I see."

Abigail's voice startled Eliza. She dropped the journal to the floor and quickly poked it back into a basket under the stand by the bed. She grabbed the copy of *Little Women* and looked up as if nothing had happened at all. "Yes, in fact I did. This looks like a great novel," she said, standing and brushing off her dress. "I can hardly wait to get started on it."

Watching her closely, Abigail wondered what Eliza had been reading. No doubt snooping into Gramma's things. Abigail shrugged. Eliza was always up to something. As long as no one got hurt, Abigail supposed she shouldn't worry about it.

Keeping Eliza occupied and her sharp tongue silent was the important thing. Then she couldn't hurt anyone.

fourteen

Abigail peered out her bedroom window at the frosty air. The wind had swept the sky clean, and it looked like beautiful weather for a wedding. She felt almost giddy as she dressed for Christopher and Mary's big day. No doubt Katie was all giggles and curls this morning. The thought brought a smile to Abigail. The family had suffered much, and God had turned things around for them.

If only she could learn to trust in the hard times. She chided herself. After all, she hadn't really experienced hard times like some people. If she was so shallow on the little things, how would she make it through the really difficult events that were sure to come? Life wasn't always easy, but in her few years, she had seen God take care of a good many people who trusted in Him.

"Abiding joy," Gramma called it. And Gramma had it. When her husband of fifty-eight years died, God brought her joy in the sorrow. Oh, she had grieved, but through her tears, she kept saying over and over, "I'll see him again one day."

Walking to the washbasin, Abigail splashed water on her face. As she patted her skin dry with a towel, she thought further. She served the Lord, but truth be known, she wasn't wholeheartedly committed. She really didn't know what held her back. Life, she supposed. She was busy with life. There wasn't always time to ponder the Creator or read His Word. She didn't actually rebel against Him, she just, well, ignored Him.

Her hands held the towel midair. Is that what she did? Ignored Him? She hadn't thought about that until now. She certainly hadn't meant to ignore Him. The truth of the matter was she put other things first. Gramma's talk had made Abigail see some things in her own life. She wanted the deep-rooted faith of which Gramma talked, the kind that dug deep into the soil of God's love and stood strong in the thrashing winds of life.

She plopped onto the bed. *Roots stretch deep in search of water. There are twists and turns, but still they probe, ever onward, doing whatever it takes to survive.* That's it. Her heart needed living water. She needed to dig deep into God's Word, always stretching, bending, yielding to His plan to drink from the living water. As she walked with Christ on this level, she would never thirst, because her roots would grow deep. She would not topple in life's struggles.

The very idea seemed somewhat overwhelming to Abigail. She supposed it took years of service and maturity to get to that place. Like Gramma.

She shook her head and stood up, pulling out her dress for the wedding. What had made her think such deep thoughts this morning, she couldn't imagine. After all, her only problem was to choose between two handsome suitors. Thankfully, it wasn't as though she had any overwhelming concerns in her life. When she grew old like Gramma, then she'd be strong.

Until then. . .

❧

The wedding was beautiful, and Abigail couldn't have been happier for Christopher and Mary. Mary's face glowed with joy, and Katie looked cute enough to squeeze. Christopher stood strong and confident beside his new bride, and Abigail knew they would have a bright future together.

Titus was unusually quiet as they made their way back to the O'Connor homestead. She wondered if Jonathan's return to town bothered him. But of course it didn't. It wasn't as though she and Titus had any type of arrangement between them. They were friends. Maybe a little more than friends. After all, he had kissed her.

She rubbed her temples, feeling a headache coming on. Titus looked at her.

"You feeling all right?"

She nodded.

"Christopher and Mary look very happy."

"Yes, they do," she agreed, knowing he was struggling to make small talk. She decided to help. "How is Jenny getting along?"

Talk of Jenny always made him smile. "She's doing well. Saying more words every day. I haven't seen Ma this happy in a long time." He turned to her, a look of gratitude on his face.

"I'm happy for Jenny. . .and thankful for you."

Abigail felt his gaze on her. He seemed to study her a moment. She shifted in her seat.

"When is Jonathan leaving?" he asked.

She turned to him. "He's leaving next Saturday."

Titus nodded.

"Why do you ask?"

"No reason."

They lapsed into silence once again. Since Jonathan's arrival, things had definitely grown strained between them. Abigail didn't know how to fix things just yet. How could she, when she couldn't untangle her own emotions? She didn't know how she felt about anyone these days and grew tired of thinking about it.

Titus pulled the wagon into their yard.

"We have time to eat lunch before going to Gramma's. You hungry?" Abigail asked.

He shook his head. "Don't have much of an appetite today."

With the way he looked at her, Abigail felt somehow responsible. "I won't be long."

After lunch, Eliza had decided to join Abigail on her trip to Gramma's, which surprised Abigail. Eliza always seemed bored, so Abigail assumed she'd stay home and work on her needlepoint. But today, she was different. Almost perky. Abigail couldn't help but wonder what she was up to this time.

Gramma waited with open arms when they arrived. Abigail

knew Gramma looked forward to these visits as much as she did. When she and Eliza stepped through the door, Abigail could smell the tea, the aroma lifting from the teapot on the table.

In no time they had settled into their chairs and talked of the wedding and the Doyle family's future together. Once Eliza finished her tea, she excused herself to Gramma's room to read *Little Women*. It seemed she liked sitting in there on the rocking chair, away from the noise of discussion. Gramma consented.

"I don't know how to reach her," Abigail finally whispered to Gramma after Eliza left the room.

"She is hurting, she is. I'm afraid me son has put his child through a lot." Gramma shook her head. "His rebellion against the Lord has brought grief to his family."

"I want to care about her, Gramma, but sometimes she isn't easy to love," Abigail confessed.

Gramma shrugged. "The Lord, He must feel that way about us at times," she said thoughtfully.

Abigail felt chastised. Once again, Gramma was right.

"Any decision yet on ye handsome suitors?"

Abigail shook her head. "Jonathan is still pressuring me. Titus has withdrawn, so I'm not sure of his feelings at all anymore. Maybe he's not interested."

Gramma took a swallow of tea and shook her head. "I'm not thinking so. He probably feels a trifle displaced with Jonathan here and all." She stirred more sugar into her tea. "'Tis hard to see the competition at work." Gramma winked.

"Please keep praying. I want to do the right thing. I just don't know what that is."

"I think ye mind is made up already."

"You do?" Gramma's wisdom tickled Abigail. "And just what have I decided?"

"Ye will choose Titus."

Abigail laughed. "How do you know?"

Gramma lifted a gnarled finger. "I've been around a good

many days." She tapped the side of her temple with her finger. " 'Tis ye heart that tells me."

Abigail stared at her, considering her words. "I wish it would tell me," she said with a halfhearted laugh.

"Would ye be listening?"

Abigail sat in silence. After a little while, she could finally see the truth. "You're right, Gramma. Why couldn't I see it before?"

"Perhaps ye are afraid of Titus's feelings now, since he has pulled away. Perhaps ye think if ye let Jonathan go, ye will be alone."

Abigail looked down, nodding her head. "Yes, I hadn't realized that until this very moment."

Gramma got up from her place and hobbled over to sit by Abigail. She clutched Abigail's hands with her own. "Then ye know what ye must do, Abigail."

Tears spilled onto her dress. She nodded once more.

"Me prayers will cover ye, wee one." Gramma placed a kiss on Abigail's temple. "He will give ye strength."

Huddled together, Gramma led in a prayer for direction and strength. Once she finished, Abigail's heart felt lighter. Though she didn't know how she would tell Jonathan her decision, she knew it's what she had to do.

With the matter settled, Abigail stood. "Thank you, Gramma, once again, for showing me things I don't know myself."

Gramma smiled.

Abigail headed to Gramma's room and found Eliza reading a newspaper. She jumped. Abigail wondered why Eliza appeared nervous lately. "You ready to go?"

Eliza nodded. Abigail noticed Eliza slipped two books into her bag. She wondered why Eliza needed two books. They would be back before long; she could pick the second one up then. She shrugged it off. Maybe Eliza wasn't coming the next time. Oh well, Abigail felt weary from the day's discussions. "Let's go."

❧

Friday morning after breakfast, Abigail took one more look out her window. A thin mist of frost covered rooftops. The air was white with falling snow. It seemed a perfect day for ice-skating. She wished Jonathan hadn't invited Eliza and Titus to go along. With her mind made up to say good-bye to Jonathan, seeing Titus and Eliza together would be all the harder. Pulling on her winter woolens, she glanced once more around her bedroom to make sure she had everything she needed. She did. With that, she turned and walked out of the room, setting out for the stairway.

Eliza left her room at the same time, both arriving at the stairway together. "Good morning, Eliza."

"Abigail."

They walked the wooden stairs together, the wood creaking beneath their feet. Eliza adjusted the gloves on her hands. "So you must be unhappy with Jonathan's soon departure."

Abigail knew Eliza well enough to know she was digging for information.

"I will miss him, but he has to return to work."

Eliza nodded. "And you will not return with him?"

Abigail looked at her in surprise. "Of course not. What made you think so?"

"Oh, I just assumed."

"It's not like that between us."

"Oh?" She stopped a moment. "Pity," Eliza finally said, skipping down the last two stairs and moving toward the door as if to avoid further conversation now that she'd found out what she wanted to know.

The very idea annoyed Abigail to no end. She knew Eliza's plan. To win Titus's affections. Period. The thought threw Abigail into a huff. It's not as though he were a toy to be tossed about between the two of them.

"Good-bye," Abigail called toward her mother, who sat reading the newspaper at her chair in front of the fireplace. Folding the paper, she walked over to Abigail and kissed her cheek.

"You children have a wonderful time."

Eliza smiled, and Abigail hugged her mother good-bye. Eliza and Abigail then slipped through the door into a winter wonderland.

Jonathan and Titus both greeted them. Abigail detected a hint of tension, though she wondered if she imagined it. "You ready to go?" Jonathan's face sparkled. He reached toward Abigail almost possessively to assist her into the carriage he had borrowed from a friend. She felt a little embarrassed by his behavior. The morning was perfect, though, and she didn't want to spoil it. She kept her thoughts light.

Titus helped Eliza in the back seat. Everyone settled in for a pleasant ride.

"How is Jenny doing, Titus?" Abigail turned back to him in time to see Eliza snuggle close beside him. Eliza tossed a victory smile.

"Doing better every day. She misses you, though. Wants to know if you're coming over today." He shifted an inch away from Eliza. She scooted closer. "I wasn't sure since we were going ice-skating."

Jonathan shot Abigail a look of disapproval.

"Well, I guess we'll have to wait and see how tired we all are after this morning," she said with a forced chuckle. She turned back around. With a slight attitude, she smoothed her skirts. After all, she did not appreciate Jonathan's pushiness. Perhaps he had forgotten, but he had walked out on her, not the other way around.

She would not be pushed.

Once they arrived, they all climbed out of the carriage and headed toward a bench to put on their skates. The pond was full of people once again. It was the most popular place to skate when the water iced over. It seemed to freeze faster than the other spots in town. Much safer.

Though frustrated with the men in her life, Abigail had to admit she was excited about ice-skating. She hadn't gone in quite some time and looked forward to it. While she waited for Eliza to finish strapping her ice-skates over her shoes, Abigail glanced up to watch the other skaters. A light snow drifted all around, adding the perfect touch to the scene. Bundled in heavy wraps, the crowd gracefully moved along, the sounds of their blades cutting into the ice, leaving iced shavings behind. Childish squeals and laughter filled the air as one or more spilled upon the frozen ground, causing others to pile one on the other.

Abigail laughed.

"You ready to give it a try?" Titus asked, surprising her. He reached out a hand. She dared not look at Jonathan but rather grabbed Titus's waiting hand. Before Eliza or Jonathan could protest, Titus helped her onto the pond, and they were soon drifting around the sidelines with the greatest of ease.

"They'll never forgive you, you know," Abigail said, daring to give him a sideways glance.

He looked her full in the face and laughed. "I know."

She bit her lip and couldn't help the excitement bubbling up inside her. For now, she wouldn't care about what they thought. She would enjoy the pure pleasure of the moment. "I didn't know you were such a good skater," she said.

He shrugged. "I came here a lot as a kid." He looked at her. "I wanted to say the same thing about you."

"I came here, too. You were probably the boy who always bumped into me when I was little, forcing me to get up and try again."

Titus chuckled. "I knew you weren't a quitter. Even then."

They laughed together. He put his arm around her back and escorted her around the pond at a fast pace. She wondered if Titus did that so Jonathan couldn't catch them. The sides of her bonnet flipped back with the breeze. The cold air pricked her skin, filling her with delight. Their laughter joined the others' and mingled into the air. For the moment, Abigail forgot all problems and responsibilities. She was a little girl again, caught in the rapture of the moment.

After a while, Titus slowed his pace and pulled her aside to rest. He looked into her face, his eyes twinkling. "You all right?"

Quite out of breath, she stopped laughing a moment and tried to calm herself. Her teeth smarting from the cold, she closed her mouth and breathed through her nose. "It was wonderful!" she said finally. Truth was, she hadn't felt so alive in a very long time.

"Good," he said, staring into her eyes.

Just then, Eliza and Jonathan skated up to them, neither looking quite happy.

"Well, I trust you had a nice lap or two around the pond, Abigail," Jonathan said, his glare evident to all. Titus cleared his throat and glanced at Abigail. For some reason, she wanted to giggle. Suddenly, Jonathan seemed the harsh taskmaster, and she and Titus had been like two schoolkids sneaking away for a moment of mischief.

She caught Titus's gaze. He winked at her, then turned to Eliza. "So, Eliza, do you care to go around?"

Eliza lifted her chin and threw a triumphant look to Abigail. "Certainly, Titus," she said to him, then glanced once more at Abigail before disappearing into the crowd.

Abigail watched them a moment, still smiling in spite of herself.

"Well, I don't see what is so funny, Abigail." Jonathan looked as mad as a March hare.

"What, Jonathan?"

"After all, you came here with me."

"I came here with everyone, Jonathan," she said, giving his tirade little notice.

"I see. Are you giving me your answer this way, Abigail?"

She looked at him with a start. His eyes had softened, sadness replacing his angry stare. As much as she hated to do so, she decided this was as good a time as any.

"I'm sorry, Jonathan."

"I thought as much." He stared at the pond's floor. "I brought it on myself. I should never have left."

Her hand touched his arm. "No, Jonathan, it was right that you left. It's better we know now how things really are between us so we can move on with our lives."

His proud jaw lifted. "I see you certainly have." His words were biting, but she understood. She had felt the very same when he went back east. "I hope you and Titus have a happy life together."

His words jolted her. Would they have a life together? She could only hope.

fifteen

After talking with Jonathan, Abigail felt the ice-skating was pretty much ruined. She loved Jonathan in a special way and didn't want to hurt him for the world, yet she couldn't deny her feelings. What they had shared was a wonderful friendship, not love. She could see that now. Though she didn't know what the future held for her and Titus, she knew her future was not with Jonathan. Still, she didn't want to hurt him.

After a quiet drive home, Titus and Eliza got out of the carriage, and Jonathan stayed with Abigail. "I'm sorry it didn't work out, Abigail."

Tears sprang to her eyes. "Me, too, Jonathan."

"You're sure?" He lifted her chin, causing their eyes to meet. She swallowed hard, tears trailing down her cheeks. "I'm sure," she said.

"If I thought I could change your mind, I'd stick around, you know. Give up my job, everything."

She looked at him. "Please, Jonathan, don't do that."

He shook his head. "No, I won't. We both know there's no future." He looked toward the barn. "I wonder if Titus Matthews knows what a lucky man he is?"

Her breath stuck in her throat.

"I will never forget you, Abigail O'Connor." His finger wiped the tears from her cheeks. Like the quick brush of the wind, his lips lit softly upon where the tears had been, then he got down and helped her from the carriage. Once they arrived at the door, Abigail turned to him.

"Thank you, Jonathan, for being a wonderful friend. For understanding."

"Good-bye, Abigail."

"Good-bye." Abigail turned and pushed through the front door. Her parents and Eliza stood just inside, as if waiting for her. She lifted tear-stained cheeks and knew she didn't have to offer an explanation just yet. "Good night, Mother, Father." She turned to her cousin. "Eliza."

Before they could answer, her legs carried her hastily up the stairway and into her room. Barnabas followed closely behind. Abigail dropped onto her bed and buried her face in her hands. Barnabas seemed to sense her sorrow. He whined as his cold nose nudged her arm, as if wanting to comfort her. When she didn't respond, he gave up and curled up at her feet.

After a little while, she fell back against her pillow. "Good-bye, Jonathan Clark. I'm sorry," she whispered into the air before falling asleep with her tears.

❧

Titus finished feeding the horses and heard a sound at the barn door. He turned around to see Eliza standing there, holding a book. Inwardly, he cringed. Hadn't he had enough of her for one day? Right now all he wanted was time to think. Alone.

She lifted an eyebrow as she waved the book in front of him. "I've found what I've been looking for."

He didn't like the look on her face. It spelled trouble. Something he didn't need right now. He had enough confusion going on in his life.

"Look, Eliza, I'm tired and—"

She would not be put off. "You don't understand. I've discovered a family secret. A secret no one knew but Gramma and Thomas O'Connor."

Titus knew he shouldn't listen further, yet curiosity got the better of him. "All right, what is it?"

She smacked her lips like one with the juiciest bit of gossip. "Let's go over there." She pointed toward a secluded corner in the barn. Once they settled in, she pulled open the pages of Gramma's journal and began to read:

"Thomas left me house a moment ago. Me heart is heavier than 'tis ever been. What shall we do? With Lavina unable to have children, the baby on their doorstep had seemed such a miracle. Never would I have guessed such deception in me son. I knew the past year had brought ill health to him, but I hadn't realized it stemmed from guilt.

" 'Tis a business trip had led him to a night of indiscretion. A night that would bring blessing and pain. Unable to live with the guilt, Thomas surrendered his heart to Christ tonight. He came to me to help him pray. 'Tis why he revealed this hidden sin to me. Still, the blessing of it 'tis the gift of baby Abigail.

"I wondered how the child's mother could leave her baby. She didn't want the responsibility, says Thomas. He gave her money for her trouble, and she went on her way. Me heart breaks at the thought of the future. Thomas has decided it best to keep the truth from Lavina.

"After the doctor told Lavina she would never have children, despair overtook her. One day a knock sounded at their door, and she opened it to see a tiny child wrapped in warm blankets, sleeping peacefully in a basket. Lavina was convinced God had seen her distress and come to her aid. Thomas could not bring himself to hurt her once more.

"He means well, but I wonder at his wisdom in this matter. Can it ever be good to conceal a truth? I'm afraid only time will tell."

Eliza closed the book with a triumphant *snap*. Titus felt sick. He had dreamed of this day, and now that it was here, it loomed over him like a dark shadow. How could he hurt this wonderful family who had brought him into their home, treated him as a son? He couldn't deny pain still lurked and rekindled his pride, but he refused to surrender to it.

"So, when shall we bring this to light?" Eliza was asking, pulling Titus from his thoughts.

He sighed and ran fingers through his hair. "Eliza, I don't

know. I need to think on this."

She looked at him a moment. "All right, we should have a plan to get the most from this. You give it some thought, and I will, too. Then we'll meet back here in the barn tomorrow night. Will that work for you?"

He stared at her.

She placed her hands on her hips. "Well, will it?"

He knew she had him where she wanted him. She could tell the O'Connors he had been snooping in the study that day. They would piece things together as to why he was there. No matter how it turned out, he would lose. He needed to think things through, stall Eliza in any way he could.

"Yes."

Her face relaxed. "Good. It's all settled then." She turned to go.

"One thing, Eliza."

She looked back at him. "What is it?"

"When the truth is revealed and their family torn apart, where will you go?"

She smiled. "My parents will have to take me back. Where else would I go?"

"So this is about you going home?"

Her face turned hard, rigid. "It's about bringing down this goody-goody family. I'm sick of their religion, their wealth being shoved in my face." Her face contorted with every word. Titus wondered if bitterness made him look like that. "Ever since I was a child, it was always their family with the money, the happy times, while our family struggled. Just ask my father. He will tell you. He's tired of living in the shadow of his big brother. I don't blame him. I detest them all."

Titus cringed at the venom in her voice. This family didn't deserve her harsh words. Still, he couldn't fault Eliza when he had thought the same about them at one time.

But not anymore.

He nodded at her. "Tomorrow then."

"Tomorrow," she said with a gleam in her eye. She turned

and walked away. He watched her, amazed at how bitterness had taken this woman's beauty and destroyed it. Something told him his ma had seen that same look on him.

He had much to think about.

❧

The next day, Titus knew he should feel guilty about not going to the O'Connors' house, but it was the only chance he had for stalling Eliza. He stepped from his barn after feeding the horse and walked toward his house. Abigail's horse and empty wagon stood out front. His feet stopped. Had she come? With Eliza?

He took a deep breath and stepped inside. Pulling off his hat, he turned to his ma and Abigail. "Hello. Is everything all right?"

Ma cut in. "She wanted to drop off some chicken noodle soup for Jenny." With her gaze pinned on him, she added, "Since Jenny is feeling so poorly." He didn't miss her look of disapproval. Did Abigail see it? He quickly looked at Abigail, but she didn't seem to notice Ma's chastisement.

Fortunately, Jenny was taking her morning nap, so Abigail could believe his sister might be sick.

"I do hope she is feeling better soon," Abigail said, glancing at Jenny's form on her bed. "Father told me you stopped in last night and let them know you wouldn't be there today because Jenny was feeling ill, so I thought I'd bring her something."

He glanced at Ma. She still glared at him. "Thank you, Abigail. That's very kind of you."

She smiled.

"Well, it's almost lunchtime. Would you care to join us?" Ma said.

"Oh no, I couldn't do that."

"Oh yes, you could," Ma persisted.

Titus knew Ma was inviting Abigail to make him uncomfortable. One thing about it, Ma could sure be stubborn. He supposed that's why her prayers got through. No doubt the Lord got tired of her nagging.

"Well, if you put it that way," Abigail said with a laugh.

"Good. Titus, help set the table, please."

Titus threw her a wait-'til-I-get-you-alone look and commenced to set the table.

Once the meal was over and the good-byes were said, Titus walked Abigail out to the wagon. "I'm glad Jenny seems to be doing better today. Maybe lunch helped."

Titus swallowed hard. "Do you think your parents would want me to come today?"

She shook her head. "Though it's hard to get along without you, I'm sure we could manage for one day." She laughed.

"Is Jonathan leaving today?"

She looked down and nodded.

"I take it you've decided to part ways?"

With her head still bent, she answered, "Yes."

He lifted her chin in his hand. "I'm glad."

His heart turned over with the sight of her. He loved this woman and could see in her eyes that she loved him, too. He wanted her to be his wife, but their future rested in the hands of another.

Eliza O'Connor.

≈

"You want to tell me what that was all about?" Ma said when Titus went back inside.

He scratched his head and took the load from his feet, falling into a kitchen chair. Bowing his head, he stretched fingers through his hair, staring at the table.

Ma sat down nearby, her hand reaching over to him. "Titus, what is it?"

He explained the whole story to her. His life, his bitterness, his need for God, his love for Abigail, and now Eliza's scheme.

Ma thought a moment. "I see. The only solution I can see to this problem is God."

He looked at her.

"You've been running long enough, Titus. You see where your way has taken you. Our way is never the right way. God's way is always right. Now, mind you, I'm not saying everything will turn out the way you want it, but I'm saying He will help you through it."

Titus hung his head and nodded. His eyes filled with tears. He couldn't remember the last time he had cried. He thought his tears had all dried up. Ma led him in a prayer. Titus recommitted his love for the Lord and offered himself as an empty vessel for God to use as He saw fit. No matter what the consequences. Once the prayer was over, he knew things were different. He felt better, lighter.

He would face Eliza directly come Monday. He wouldn't discuss the matter at church. She'd have to wait.

Eliza did wait, though not happily so. Titus would not ruin Sunday with their talk of destroying the O'Connor family. He hoped the Lord would give him a way yet to get out of the whole ordeal. Most of all, he didn't want to hurt Abigail. Perhaps Eliza would give it up—though he knew that was about as likely as Chicago turning into a ghost town.

He was right. Come Monday morning, bright and early, Eliza stood ready to greet him at the barn when he pulled up, the journal held firmly in her hand. He prayed once again for strength and hopped from his wagon.

Bitterness pushed her forward. Her eyes lit with the thrill of hurting another. "Are you ready?"

He grabbed her hand. "Listen, Eliza, why are you bent on doing this? The O'Connors have been good to both of us, taking us in—"

She jerked her hand away. "Oh, don't tell me you're going soft!"

He blew out a frustrated sigh. "It's just that I don't see the sense in all this."

"I don't believe you. You know Uncle Thomas stood by and watched your pa go under financially. No wonder your pa had a heart attack!" Her words hurt him to the core, but he saw his old reflection in her. The bitterness had twisted and marred her face in a way he hadn't seen before on himself. But

God saw it. And He had set Titus free.

"There's a better way, Eliza. God can help us—"

She gasped. "What? You've got religion now?" She looked at him incredulously. Once again she took a proud stance. "Well, if I have to do this myself, so be it." With that, she stomped across the yard toward the house.

His stomach knotted like an old rope as he followed Eliza to the house. Chills pricked up his arm, and he broke out in a cold sweat. He hurled a frantic prayer for wisdom toward the heavens and stepped in just behind Eliza. She turned to him with surprise. The look on her face said she thought he would back her up. *God help us.*

"Oh, good, I was just going to come out for you both. Breakfast is ready," Mrs. O'Connor said. Titus felt it was more like the Last Supper.

The family took their seats at the table. Titus glanced at Abigail. Her eyes questioned him as if she knew something was amiss.

The dishes were passed, and Titus shoved eggs around on his plate, dreading what was sure to come.

"Titus, I hope you're not getting what your sister had. You've hardly touched a bite," Mrs. O'Connor said.

"Yes, ma'am."

"Well, I discovered a bit of news the last time I went to Gramma's house," Eliza offered before biting into a piece of toast.

All eyes turned to her. Mr. O'Connor spread some butter across his toast. "What might that be?" he asked in all innocence.

A smile lit her face, and she looked the happiest Titus had ever seen her. She sickened him not only because of her behavior but because she reminded him so much of himself. How God could forgive him, Titus didn't know. He only knew God had forgiven him, and he was thankful.

Just then a knock sounded at the door.

"I'll get it," Mr. O'Connor said, wiping his mouth with the cloth napkin, then laying it on the table.

Titus glanced at Eliza, who was frowning.

"You were saying, Eliza?" Mrs. O'Connor continued.

Eliza lifted her head. "Oh, nothing. It can wait. I'd rather share it with everyone here."

"Well, it seems I have to go out of town for railroad business, dear," Mr. O'Connor said upon his return to the dining room.

"Can't you finish your meal, Thomas?" his wife asked.

"No time. I've really got to run."

Mrs. O'Connor stood. "How long will you be gone?"

He shook his head. "I'm not sure. Probably about a week." His steps were already carrying him out of the room.

Titus and Eliza exchanged a glance. She huffed and stood.

"Are you all right?" Abigail wanted to know.

"Nothing a week won't cure," Eliza said with a scowl.

"I'm sorry?" Abigail asked.

"Nothing." With that, Eliza stomped out of the room.

"What's wrong with her?"

Titus shrugged but said nothing. He pushed his plate aside. "I'm going back to work," he announced before leaving Abigail alone at the table.

sixteen

"Titus, feel free to grab a cup of coffee, if you want, and come back in about an hour," Abigail said once she stepped from the carriage. It was ten o'clock, but the light fog persisted upon the city. Horses *clip-clopped* past them, with rattling buggies following close behind. Gas flames flickered from the street lamps, mingling with the haze, wrapping the street in a mysterious glow.

"You certain you won't be finished before then? I don't want to make you wait."

Abigail smiled at his consideration. "I'm certain. I need to spend some time with Sophia."

Titus turned his hat around in his hands, a familiar gesture to which Abigail had grown accustomed. "Are you all right, Titus?"

He looked at her with eyes that said he had much to say. Still, he kept silent. He finally nodded and shrugged on his hat, then turned back toward the carriage. She watched him pull away, her heart heavy. Grabbing a fistful of her skirt, she walked toward the Thread Bearer.

The bell jangled overhead as she entered. The smell of coffee drifted from the kitchen. Sophia was at her usual place in the room, head bent over a sewing machine. She looked up with surprise.

"Abigail, I'm so glad you came!" She got up and walked over to her friend.

"You did say Wednesdays around ten o'clock was a good time for you, didn't you? Is this still a convenient time for a visit?" Abigail hoped so, since she had already told Titus to leave.

"This is perfect," Sophia said. She grabbed Abigail's hand.

"Let's get some coffee and sit down for a while in the kitchen."

Abigail pulled off her wraps and settled into her chair while Sophia poured the coffee into their cups. Once they both were seated, Sophia looked at Abigail. "So, tell me what's going on in your life these days. Seems we never have time enough to talk at church."

With a nod, Abigail smiled.

"Jonathan has left?"

"Yes." Her hands hugged the coffee cup. "It wasn't the same. When we were together, things had changed. I think for both of us, though he wouldn't admit it just yet."

"I'm sorry, Abby."

She shrugged. "It's all right. I'm glad I had the chance to find it out rather than always wondering what might have been." Glancing up with a smile, she said, "We did go ice-skating."

Sophia's eyes sparkled. "Oh, you did? I haven't gone ice-skating since I went with Jonathan on your behalf ages ago. Remember, when you had to go out of town with your parents and you wanted me to keep Mary Nottinger away from him?"

They both laughed.

"I'd forgotten all about that!" Abigail took a drink of her coffee and thought a moment. "Whatever happened to Mary, anyway? I haven't seen her in a long time."

Sophia shook her head and looked away, lost in thought. "Mary. Bless her heart. Her mother, Alice, tells me Mary is off seeing the sights of Europe with a favorite aunt." Sophia took another drink, then put her cup down. "To tell you the truth, I think she was brokenhearted after your cousin Patrick left."

Abigail shook her head. "Mary pursued him like a hound after a fox, and Patrick couldn't leave town fast enough." They laughed again. "Truthfully, Patrick's job at the railroad wasn't what he wanted. He went back home." Abigail paused a moment. "But he married shortly after, so I think he just wanted to get back to the woman he loved. I think Uncle Mark and Aunt Emma were glad he came home."

"How many uncles do you have?"

"Just two. Three boys in the family; that's it."

"Only two cousins, right?"

"Right. Patrick is Uncle Mark's son, and Eliza is Uncle Edward's daughter."

A comfortable silence fell between them as they sipped on their drinks. "Are you doing all right, Abby?"

Abigail looked at Sophia. "Yes. Why do you ask?"

Sophia held her gaze. "Something seems not quite right. I can't put my finger on it."

"We really are like sisters, you know."

Sophia lifted an eyebrow. "Oh?"

"You can't put your finger on what's wrong, because I can't put a finger on it. I mean, I did the right thing by Jonathan. I love him dearly but as a friend. I see that now. And I know that I love Titus. It's just that, well, I thought he felt the same way."

"And now?"

"That's what I mean. I don't know. I once worried he had feelings for Eliza, but then I changed my mind. Yet for the past few days, he's been acting strange. I've caught him whispering in corners with Eliza, which makes me think perhaps I was wrong. Possibly he does have feelings for her, and I've misread everything."

Sophia looked at her a moment. "I can't imagine Titus falling for someone like Eliza. She doesn't seem his type at all." Sophia clasped her hands together at her chin as she listened.

"That's what I thought, but now I don't know what to think."

"I'll be praying for you, Abigail. And for Titus. Most likely, time will tell what's bothering him. How is Jenny getting along?"

Abigail felt herself lighten with the mention of the little girl. "Oh, Sophia, she is doing so well. She's pretty much back to speaking normally again. Though she doesn't talk a lot, she is able to communicate, which is better than before. I'm so proud of her."

"Sounds to me like the Lord has really used you to help that family."

She shook her head. "It has been my privilege. They have been through so much."

Sophia nodded. "Do you think Titus will ever go back to medical school?"

"I don't know. I pray for his future. I know that's his dream. I pray one day the Lord will open doors for him." Abigail picked up her cup and sipped a little more. "Now, tell me about you and Clayton and the baby. What is going on with you?"

Sophia practically glowed. "I'm happy beyond belief. I feel wonderful, and I'm counting the days 'til the baby comes." A thought seemed to hit her. "Oh, wait, I have to show you something." Sophia got up and left the room for a moment. Abigail waited, smiling at her friend's enthusiasm. She imagined her own parents' excitement when they found her on their doorstep.

Sophia came back into the room, almost out of breath. "I've finished the baby's booties." She held up tiny knitted booties and wiggled them from the ends of her fingers for Abigail to see.

"Oh, these are adorable!" Abigail ran her fingers carefully along the dainty stitches. She looked up at her friend. "I'm so happy for you, Sophia."

Sophia beamed and carefully placed the booties into a box.

Abigail glanced at the timepiece dangling from a golden chain around her neck. "Oh dear, I'd better go. Titus has been waiting ten minutes already for me."

The two friends hugged. "I will be praying for you, Abigail, and for Titus."

"Thank you. And I will be praying for you," she said, adding a pat to Sophia's stomach, "and the little one."

Sophia walked Abigail to the door and waved at Titus. He waved back and stepped over to help Abigail into the carriage.

"To Barnabas House now?" he asked.

"Yes, please." With one more glance toward the Thread

Bearer, Abigail waved good-bye to her friend, all the while thanking the Lord for Sophia and praying for their little family.

ào

No one seemed to notice Abigail as she stepped into Barnabas House. The workers were engrossed in their duties, and children sat at their table with slates in hand, carefully working out arithmetic lessons. Julie stood peering over their shoulders, checking their work. Before Abigail could reach them, Mary O'Grady's voice called behind her.

"Abigail, so good to see you!"

She turned to Mary's smiling face. "Mary O'Grady—I mean, Doyle! How are you?"

The woman blushed. "I'm thanking you for asking. We're doing just fine, that we are."

"And Katie?"

"Ah, my little lassie is happy as can be." They both looked over at the little girl. The tip of her tongue poked slightly through the corner of her mouth as she worked diligently on her slate. The women chuckled.

"I don't know how the wee one would work without the help of her tongue. Would you like some coffee?"

"No, thank you. I just came in to see when Julie needed my help. She's a hard worker."

"Aye, she is. Do you mind that she has taken over so much of the work?"

Abigail smiled. "Not at all. As you know, I've been working with Jenny Matthews."

"Aye. How is that coming along?"

Abigail explained Jenny's progress. Before they could continue, Katie's voice broke through their discussion.

"Miss Abigail!" She ran over to hug her. Katie looked up and smiled, revealing a missing tooth on the top, just right of the middle.

Abigail gasped. "Oh my, you've lost a tooth! Aren't you the lucky one!"

Katie beamed, swinging from side to side. Her fingers felt

around her neckline and she pulled out her locket for Abigail to see.

Abigail stooped down. "Oh, Katie dear, I'm so glad to see you wearing your necklace."

Without a word, Katie dropped the necklace back into place and threw her arms around Abigail. "I miss you."

"I miss you, too."

"Where's Barnabas?" Katie asked, looking around.

"He couldn't come today. I had other errands to attend to."

Katie nodded and changed the subject. "I like my new pa."

Abigail looked up at Mary, and they exchanged a smile. "He is a good pa, Katie."

"I'm working hard today." She crinkled her nose and quirked her lips into a pucker. "I don't like arithmetic much."

Abigail crinkled her nose. "I don't either. But it's one of those things we need to know." Abigail laughed and touched the tip of Katie's nose with her finger. "Now, you'd better get back to work." After one more hug, the little girl skipped back to the table.

The other children, noting her absence, looked up to see Abigail, and they waved. She smiled and returned their greeting.

"They love you, you know," Mary said.

"I know. I love them, too."

"Well, I'll be letting you talk to Julie. I wanted to say hello before you got away."

"Mary, it's good to see you so happy." Abigail could see the sparkle in the woman's eyes. Such a contrast to what she used to see there.

"Aye, God has worked a miracle for us. We'll be forever grateful."

The two women hugged once more, then Abigail made her way to Julie to see when next she would be needed to help.

ã

Titus's heart flipped when he saw Abigail step from Barnabas House. Never before had he felt this way about a woman.

And their future held together by a sliver of hope. If Eliza had her way, she would shred every chance of happiness from everyone in her path. He had never seen a woman with such a bent toward evil. Before he could allow his harsh judgment of her to run rampant, he remembered she was no different from what he had been before the Lord cleansed him. God could do the same for Eliza. Titus needed to pray for her.

In the meantime, what would become of Abigail? Her family? *Please, God, protect them from Eliza's evil scheme.*

"Thank you for waiting, Titus," Abigail was saying when she stepped up to the carriage.

"My pleasure, Abby." She looked at him with a start. He could have kicked himself. Why had he called her that? It had slipped from his tongue before he could stop it. Though he had called her that a thousand times in his dreams, he had never used so familiar a name when addressing her before. "I'm sorry," he corrected himself.

She touched his arm. "Don't be. I like it."

How he wanted to pull her into his arms and kiss her like before. Would they ever know a moment like that again? He started to lift her into the carriage, and she hesitated a moment. Her eyes looked up to him. "Titus, is everything all right?"

He swallowed hard. "Yes. Why?"

"You've just seemed a little, well, distant, in the past few days. Jenny is all right, isn't she?"

Her worried eyes melted his heart. As always, she worried about someone else. So unlike Eliza. "Jenny is fine."

"And you?"

How he wanted to tell her the truth before Eliza could spread her poison, but he didn't know where to start or what to say. Would she forgive him for his original intention of wanting to get back at her family? Would she believe he had changed?

"Titus?" Her questioning eyes bore into him.

He sighed. "I'm fine, Abigail. Really." He didn't want to lie to her, but the setting wasn't right. He could hardly go into the entire story while standing at the side of the road with buggies and people walking about. Still, how could he be anything less than honest? "Maybe sometime soon we can talk." There, he let her know something was amiss, he just didn't go into what it was.

Her questioning eyes met his once again. "I'd like that." She lifted her hand so he might help her into the carriage. The mere touch of her hand made him weak-kneed. No doubt about it, he had to talk to her. He couldn't live with himself until she knew the truth. Better he talk to her before Eliza did. Eliza would hold nothing back. She would spit the truth out, making it as bleak and ugly as possible.

No, he couldn't let that happen. He had to talk to Abigail first chance they got. Hopefully, he could get to her before Eliza.

seventeen

It was midmorning on Saturday before Titus could get Abigail alone. He was careful not to let Eliza see them for fear she would get jealous and spill the news in a fit of anger. When Abigail slipped from the house into the barn, he had the wagon hitched and ready to go.

"Now, Titus, tell me what all this secrecy is about," Abigail said with a chuckle. How he hated to reveal the truth and shatter her happiness.

"I'd rather take you somewhere, Abigail, just the two of us, and talk about it."

"All I know is this has something to do with Eliza, and you're not going to give me even a hint as to what else?"

He smiled at her, trying to keep her at ease. "You'll find out soon enough." His finger trailed her cheekbone. "Just remember, things aren't always as they seem." She studied him. He reached over to help her into her seat when he heard the rattling of a carriage. He looked up to see Mr. O'Connor returning home from his trip. Abigail dashed across the yard with the excitement of a child.

Mr. O'Connor's arrival struck Titus with a heavy blow. For in that moment, Titus realized he was too late.

He slipped back into the barn while the family came out to greet Mr. O'Connor. Their happy murmurings drifted into the barn as he tried to sort the matter through in his mind.

"You coming in?" Eliza's words sliced through the air.

His head jerked up to see her standing in front of him; a face hard as a wagon wheel looked at him. "They're fixin' to sit down to some lunch."

"It's not quite time for lunch."

"Probably just coffee and a pastry or two. Something to

celebrate Uncle's return." Eliza laughed. "We'll have something to celebrate, all right." She turned to go.

Titus grabbed her arm. "Eliza, I beg you, don't do this."

She sneered at him. "You're crazy as a loon if you think I'm giving this up after all my planning."

"I don't care beans about all your planning. By hurting this family, you accomplish nothing."

"Oh, I accomplish something, all right."

"They have done nothing but extend kindness to you. For that you hate them?"

She jerked her arm free. "What would you know? You're merely their chauffeur. You're soft because of Abigail." She snapped the name off her tongue as if it were poison. "You know nothing of our family history. They blame my father for everything. But I know different. I've heard his side of the story."

"That's right, you've heard his side, and you've allowed it to poison your mind, Eliza. Your father is wrong. If this family is so bad and he's such a wonderful father, why would he leave you with them? You might as well face it, Eliza, your father is a snake!"

Before he could blink, she reached her arm back and slapped him across the face. He stared at her in disbelief. She stepped back, as if shocked by her own action. Without another word, she turned and ran to the house.

He had provoked her, and he knew for that he would pay. Most likely, so would the O'Connors.

⁊

Once the chatter of Mr. O'Connor's trip and the excitement of having him home once again died down, Mrs. O'Connor passed around the pastries and filled the coffee cups.

Titus's stomach gurgled as nausea filled him. Not knowing when Eliza planned to attack made him weak. Finally, in the quiet of the moment as they passed the pastry plate, she struck like a venomous snake.

"Oh, did I tell you the last time I was at Gramma's house

that I found her journal?" She took a bite of pastry and looked at them with a smile, seeming to enjoy their shocked expressions. Titus noticed Thomas O'Connor's face turned pale.

"Honestly, Eliza, I don't think you should be snooping into Gramma's personal belongings," Abigail said.

"That's right, dear. A journal is very personal. People don't mean to share their words with others," Mrs. O'Connor added.

Eliza chewed slowly, as if to draw out the matter. Titus wished her father had taken her to the woodshed as a child. Better still, he wished Mr. O'Connor would do it now. She reached under the table and pulled out the journal. With slow motions, she pulled it open. "Hmm, it says here," she moved her tongue around her teeth as if to stall further, then smacked her lips together. "Um, let's see." She ran her finger along the page. "Oh yes, here it is."

Titus braced himself. Slowly, with great deliberation, she read the revealing words, accentuating those words that would bring the most pain. Her tongue sliced its way into their souls, like the cut of a deadly blade. After all was read, they sat in a cold silence.

Tears rolling down her cheeks, Mrs. O'Connor looked at Eliza. "Why did you tell us this?"

"Oh," she said with a wave of her hand, "Titus and I thought it would be a good idea. After all you've done for the two of us, separating me from my father and, of course, separating Titus from his father."

Abigail looked at him with the greatest sorrow he had ever seen on the face of another. Her eyes filled with tears. His tongue refused to move, knowing no words could salve the pain for any of them. She got up from the table and ran to her room. Mrs. O'Connor quickly followed.

Eliza continued to eat as though nothing had happened.

"Mr. O'Connor, I—" Titus tried to explain, but Thomas O'Connor held up his hand. The older man turned to Eliza. "I will write your father, Eliza. You can take the first train home. I'm certain that's what you had hoped for, anyway." She offered a smile, but one look at Titus erased the smile from her face.

Titus stood to his feet, hat in hand. "I'm sorry, Mr. O'Connor. Truly sorry." He walked out the front door and didn't look back.

❧

The O'Connor family managed to get through Sunday with little conversation. No one spoke of Eliza's news. Rather they talked of surface things, attended church together, then hurried home to retreat behind closed doors.

On Monday morning, Abigail opened her eyes to the sound of muffled cries and looked into her mother's tear-stained face.

"I'm leaving, dear. Just for a little while," she whispered, using her fingers to brush aside Abigail's hair from her face.

Abigail gasped and sat up in the bed. "What will I do, Mother?"

"You'll be fine. Your father has gone to work, but I've left him a note. He'll need you to see after him. You're old enough to understand that I need time to think, sort things through. I love your father desperately, but I'm struggling with his deception. I can hardly bear it."

"Where will you go, Mother?"

"I'm going to visit an old friend. She lives on Nantucket Island and recently lost her husband. I suppose the time near the sea will do me good, though it's cold this time of year. Perhaps I can help her through her grief. Still, I don't know that I'll be of any good."

Abigail started to cry. "How long will you be gone?"

Her mother looked away. "I'm afraid I don't know. Pray for me."

"I feel like this is all my fault." Abigail pulled her hands up to her face.

Mother's attention jerked back to her. "Oh my, no! You have been the dearest thing to me. An answer to my prayers. I never doubted God used you to restore joy to my life."

"Yet now you want to leave."

"It's not you I'm leaving, dear." Mother smoothed Abigail's hair.

"You would leave Father. But hasn't he suffered in silence for all these years? You heard the words of Gramma's journal—he wanted to spare you the pain."

Mother thought a moment. "Yes, I know. Still, knowing he betrayed my love and lived a lie all these years. . ." Her words trailed off.

"But he didn't know the Lord when he committed the sin."

"Yes, but he knew me." Fresh tears began to flow.

Abigail squeezed her mother's arms. "It was so long ago. Can't you forgive him?"

"I want to, Abigail. I truly do."

"But you've talked to me endless times about forgiving others. Even forgiving Jonathan for the pain he caused me."

Mother nodded. She looked her daughter full in the face. "Perhaps I never fully understood your pain because I've never had to forgive such a betrayal of trust. I've never known such pain, Abigail. The strength to forgive must come from God. I cannot find it in me."

The two women embraced. Abigail allowed her tears to flow. "Please, don't go."

"Pray for me. I will pray for you."

After one more hug, Mother turned from Abigail's room and collected her things. Mother waited by the door for Titus to bring the carriage around. Abigail stood nearby but couldn't bring herself to say another word. She knew her mother's mind was made up.

When Titus finally knocked at the front door, Abigail jumped. "Mother?"

Her mother turned to her. "Pray, Abigail. Pray for us all." With that, her mother walked out the door and out of her life. For how long, Abigail didn't know. She prayed that one day her mother would return. And that her father would be waiting.

Titus carried out some luggage, then returned for the last piece. Abigail lifted it and handed it to him. Their eyes met for a moment. His face was red and swollen with dirt streaked across his cheek. His eyes begged for understanding.

A lump grew in Abigail's throat, and she could say nothing. She could only stand and watch as he turned and walked away, and the carriage once again prepared to take away someone she loved.

Two someones.

With a flick of the reins, Titus had the team up and trotting. Abigail stood in the doorway and watched them fade into the flurry of snow. She glanced at the heavy gray clouds looming overhead. Fresh snowflakes fell to the ground, covering the crusty, cold earth beneath. A thought intruded and surprised her. God's love did that for her. Made her black heart pure as new-fallen snow.

Though Abigail had no idea how this would all turn out, her heavy heart quickened with the reminder that God was in control. Barnabas rubbed against her legs, pushing his nose into her skirts. She patted him twice on the head; he licked the top of her hand and snuggled some more.

With a sigh, Abigail closed the door, then turned toward the shell of what had once been a home. A home ringing with laughter and joy.

Walking toward the kitchen, Abigail decided she'd better make plans for dinner.

Later that evening, Eliza elected to eat her meal in her room. The next morning's train would carry her home.

Father ate a little dinner with Abigail, though neither had much to say. After their meal, Abigail went into the drawing room and settled by the fire, mending some clothes. Father joined her, reading the newspaper. After a little while, he folded the paper and laid it on the floor beside him.

"Abigail, might we talk?"

She looked up and nodded, carefully laying aside her needle and thread.

"I was wrong. I thought I had done the right thing by keeping this from your mother, but I was wrong." He pulled his hands to the sides of his head. "Oh, how I wish I could wipe that painful sin from my life." She watched him agonize with the pain of it. She walked over to him and knelt by his feet. Lifting red, weary eyes, he grabbed her hand. "I'm thankful for you, child, but I loathe myself for the sin I've committed."

"I know, Father. But God has forgiven you."

"God has forgiven me, but what if your mother cannot?"

Abigail didn't have the answer for that.

"I don't know what I'll do if she doesn't return," Father said, tears running down his face. Abigail had never seen her father cry before. She touched his shoulder.

"Mother loves you, and she knows deep down that you love her."

He looked at her through red, watery eyes and merely patted her hand. He struggled to his feet. Bent and weary, he shuffled out of the room, looking much older to Abigail than she had ever seen him.

The next morning, Eliza had her bags packed and ready to go by the time Titus came to the door. Abigail stepped up behind her cousin.

"Eliza?" Abigail said.

She turned around with a start. "Yes?" Her stance showed her bracing herself for anything Abigail might throw her way.

Abigail wanted to show her anger, to hurl pain upon her cousin for all she had done to Abigail's family, but with one look at Eliza, Abigail changed her mind. "I–I wish things could have been different," was all she said. To Abigail's amazement, she meant it. Expecting an unkind retort, Abigail was surprised to instead find a look of sorrow flash across Eliza's face.

Eliza gave a slight nod. So slight, Abigail almost missed it.

Perhaps God had not given up on Eliza.

❧

When Titus showed up for work on Tuesday morning, Abigail heard her father talking to him.

"Titus, I thought we had an understanding. I never knew the depths of the hatred that simmered in your heart. For that I am dreadfully sorry. I cannot fix the past, nor can I undo what happened to your pa. I had hoped to help you, but not from a guilty heart, as I'm sure you supposed. Rather out of a heart of respect for the friendship I had shared with your pa." He blew out a sigh of regret. "Knowing you feel as you do, I suspect it's best you leave your position with us."

"But I don't feel that way, sir, I—"

The older man held up his hand. "I need time, Titus, to think this through. You understand?"

"Yes, sir," was all Titus said. His head drooped, and he walked away. A sharp pain went through Abigail's chest. She struggled to ignore it. How could she feel soft toward this man who had used her affections and worked side by side with Eliza to bring the O'Connor family to ruin?

Abigail had renewed her vows to the Lord, making every effort to give Him first place in her life. She knew now that in order to please her heavenly Father, she must forgive, but like her mother, she didn't have the strength on her own. Only after much prayer would she find the strength. And even then she might be able to forgive, but she now knew there would never be a future together for her and Titus.

That brought to Abigail the worst pain of all.

eighteen

By Wednesday afternoon, the silence in the house made Abigail restless. She decided to go to Gramma's house. She wasn't there very long before she crumbled in a heap.

"Gramma, everything is terrible." Abigail wiped her nose for the hundredth time on her handkerchief. "Our family will never be the same."

"There, there, Abigail darling," Gramma said, patting Abigail's hand. "We will get through this, we will." Gramma looked away. " 'Tis Eliza I'm worried about, I am."

Abigail jerked her head toward Gramma with a start. "Why ever would you worry about her? She brought this disaster to our home."

"No," Gramma was saying. " 'Tis your father's sin brought this about. Eliza merely made the hidden sin known." Gramma thought some more. "I shouldn't have written about it in a journal. What was I thinking? Someone would have surely found it after I was gone." She shrugged. "I'd forgotten I'd even written the words. So very long ago."

"It's not your fault, Gramma."

"No. No. Your father committed the sin, and he should have told your mother. Still, he thought he was doing the best thing by her." Gramma looked away again. " 'Tis all so tragic."

"Why do you worry about Eliza?"

Gramma stood and hobbled over to her chair. With great effort she lowered herself to within inches of the seat and finally fell into the soft cushions with a great *plop*. "Oh dear, me body doesn't cooperate like it used to." Once she settled in, she looked at Abigail. "I worry about Eliza because she has to live with herself. She knows she hurt everyone." Gramma brushed her hand in front of her. "I know she acts tough as an old cowhide, but she's not. Inside, she's still a little girl who wants her father's approval, that she does."

Abigail thought a moment. She hadn't considered that side of Eliza. Truth be known, Abigail didn't want to consider it. She wanted to be angry with Eliza for hurting her family. Yet Abigail knew Gramma was right.

"Do you think Uncle Edward and Aunt Elizabeth are able to take her back?" Abigail asked, smoothing a curl with her fingers.

A pained expression shadowed Gramma's face. "I don't know. Edward can be quite harsh at times."

"What about Aunt Elizabeth? Wouldn't she help her own daughter?"

Gramma offered a weak smile. "Elizabeth is a dear woman, but I'm afraid she's as spoiled as Edward. I'm sorry to say they never should have had children. Eliza has been the one to suffer."

Remorse settled over Abigail. She had only considered her own pain, not Eliza's. Abigail didn't want to feel sorry for Eliza. Yet what if the tables had been turned and Abigail was the one who grew up with Uncle Edward and Aunt Elizabeth? Would she have turned out like Eliza? Here she had thought she never wanted to see Eliza again, and now she wondered if she shouldn't contact her once things settled down. If they ever did.

"I've been harsh in my thoughts about Eliza," Abigail admitted. "She hurt me, and she hurt my family."

Gramma nodded. "Aye, that she did. And it's natural ye would feel hurt."

Before Abigail could comment further, someone knocked at the front door. "I'll get it," Abigail said as she rose and walked over to the door. As she opened the door, she looked at the visitor and gasped.

"May I come in?" asked their guest in a weak voice. Abigail stepped aside.

In walked Eliza O'Connor.

Abigail could hardly keep herself from gaping at Eliza as she moved into the room. "Gramma, am I welcome to come in?"

The small voice surprised Abigail. She had never seen Eliza so vulnerable.

"Of course, dear," Gramma said, motioning to a chair in which Eliza could sit.

Eliza pulled off her outer wraps and sat down. She kept her head bowed. "I couldn't do this." She pulled her hands to her face and started sobbing. Her body heaved with the weight of her burden. Abigail stood silently nearby, not knowing what to do. Gramma went over to Eliza.

After a lengthy time of tears, she finally calmed herself. "I had time to think before the train arrived. I was angry with my father and mother for making me leave. They blamed it on finances, but truth be known, they don't want a spinster daughter holding them back. You see, I received word from a friend that my parents went to Europe. They shipped me off to your family to get rid of me."

Eliza's fingers nervously toyed with the handkerchief in her hands. "I resented your family for taking me." She looked at Abigail. "Though it was a kindness, I refused to see it that way." She looked away and hiccupped, attempting to hold back more tears. "But when I thought of leaving, all I could think about was Uncle Thomas and Aunt Lavina and. . ." Once more Eliza looked up at Abigail. "And you." She shook her head and wiped her nose on the handkerchief. Her gaze was fixed on her lap. "I was jealous of you, just like my father has always been jealous of Uncle Thomas. I've allowed my father's words to poison my thoughts. Your family did not deserve what I did." She lifted tear-filled eyes to Abigail. "Will you ever forgive me?"

A flood of compassion swept over Abigail, surprising her. Her heart filled with forgiveness. The Lord had once again intervened. She went to her cousin's side. "Yes, Eliza, I forgive you." The two women hugged through their tears. When they parted, Gramma joined them with tears of joy.

"Well, this calls for some tea," Gramma announced, wiping away her tears. In no time at all, the three had prepared the tea and brought it with them into the living room. They settled comfortably into their chairs.

"Since you missed your train yesterday, what did you do last night?" Abigail asked.

After taking a drink of tea, Eliza carefully placed the cup on the saucer on a nearby stand. "I stayed in the hotel nearby to sort through things. I knew I could catch another train. I just couldn't leave things the way they were." She twisted her handkerchief in her hands. "I've behaved abominably; I know that."

"How did ye get the money for ye train trip, Eliza?" Gramma asked, stirring sugar into her tea.

Eliza smiled. "I saved some money while living at home. I took it with me, not knowing what the future would hold for me with my father practically throwing me out of the house."

They sat silent for a moment.

"I don't know what you will think of this idea, Abigail, but I have enough money that I think we could go together to Nantucket and fetch Aunt Lavina."

Abigail's eyebrows rose. "Really?"

Eliza nodded enthusiastically.

"I have a little money of my own I could contribute." Abigail turned to Gramma. "Do you think she would come?"

Gramma thought a moment. "I don't know. I'd hate for ye to get all the way out there and her not come."

"We've got to try, Gramma," Abigail said.

"I think ye would be best to wait at least a week or two. Give her time to think. Take time to pray about the matter. Then the two of ye do what ye think ye must," Gramma said.

They all decided that's just what they would do.

❧

Friday night, Titus shuffled across the porch of their home and stumbled into the house. Exhausted from searching for employment but finding none, he fought hard against the despair threatening to overtake him.

"Titus," Ma said as he entered. The kitchen chair scuffed hard against the wooden floor as she grabbed it and pulled it over to him. "Are you all right?" She lifted his hat from his head, smoothed some hair from his forehead, and looked into his eyes. "You're pushing too hard, Titus. Have you eaten today?" Before he could answer, she continued, "Day after day you don't eat. You must eat, Son. You need your strength."

Titus looked up at her. He knew she was right, but he had no appetite. How could he eat when the woman he loved would have nothing to do with him? Worry lines etched Ma's eyes. He grabbed her hand. "I'm all right, Ma."

She would not be dissuaded. "You didn't answer me. Have you eaten today?"

He smiled. "You're too smart for me."

"Oh, Titus." She dropped his hand, picked up a plate, and began to pile on the evening's meal for him. Once his plate was full of chicken, potatoes, and a biscuit, she put it in front of him. She poured hot coffee into a cup and set it down, along with a glass of water.

"Thanks, Ma." He bowed his head in prayer.

The chair groaned as she sat down across from him. "You will find work, Titus. The Lord will provide," she said after he finished his prayer.

He nodded, then took a bite of potatoes. She looked at him as if she wanted to say something, then hesitated. "What is it, Ma?"

"You've heard nothing from the O'Connors?"

He shook his head. "They never want to see me again."

"They just need time, Titus." Her eyes searched his face.

"No, Ma, I haven't heard from Abigail. She wants nothing to do with me." He knew Ma couldn't understand the depths of Abigail's pain. Pain he had caused.

"You must see her again."

He didn't look up. "Not likely. She's pretty much finished her work with Jenny. She doesn't need to come around anymore."

"You must."

"And why is that?" He glanced up at her. She sat smiling, holding one of the books she used with Jenny.

"Because you have to return this to her."

Titus looked at his ma and shook his head. A tiny smile slowly lifted the corners of his mouth.

* * *

Titus blew out a sigh. He could hardly believe four weeks had passed. Sophia had told him Abigail was out of town but hadn't offered any other information. The construction work he had obtained kept him busy but not too busy to think of Abigail. He didn't know if she had returned, but he had to find out. Reaching his hand out on the seat beside him, he patted Abigail's book.

As Titus neared the O'Connors' home, he looked at the neighboring lawns. Fresh buds poked through forgotten stems stretching toward the warmth of the sun. Still, winter's chill persisted.

A thread of cold ran through him, though he didn't know if it was the cool air or thoughts of Abigail that made him shiver. How could things go so wrong in such a short time? His scheming fell away, and for that he was thankful. But his plans with Abigail, well, they would never be. He had to let them go. The book on the seat beside him was his only hope. If he didn't see her now, he wouldn't have another excuse to drop by her house. Maybe she would refuse to see him, anyway. Her father might order Titus off their property. He hadn't thought of that. The closer he got to their homestead, the more he regretted his decision to come. His mind told him to turn around, to get home as fast as he could. His heart told him to keep going.

His heart won out.

When he reached their home, he took a deep breath, grabbed the book, and jumped out of the wagon. He looked around the place. Everything was quiet. He glanced at the barn and could see Mr. O'Connor was home. Most likely,

Abigail would be with him if she was back in town. He glanced at his pocket watch. They would have eaten half an hour ago.

Walking to the steps, he took off his hat, prayed quickly for strength and the right words, then knocked on the door. He was unprepared for what he saw when it opened.

Before him stood Thomas O'Connor, who only a few weeks before had reminded him of a mighty oak tree, tall, sturdy, rugged. Today, he looked old, tired, and spent. "Yes, Titus, what can I do for you?"

Titus held the book in his hand. He looked at it, then back to Mr. O'Connor. "I wanted to return this to Abigail."

Mr. O'Connor reached for the book.

"Is she home, sir?"

Mr. O'Connor shook his head. "I'm afraid not. She and Eliza got it in their heads to go after Lavina on their own. I was on a business trip. When I returned, I found a note telling me where they had gone."

"Eliza?"

Mr. O'Connor scratched his head. "Yeah, that surprised me, too. Don't know what that's about." He looked at Titus for a moment. "Why don't you come in?"

"Well. . ." Titus hesitated.

"Come on. I could use the company."

"All right," Titus found himself saying. He stepped into the house. Barnabas's tail wagged furiously, as if remembering Titus as an old friend. Titus reached down and patted the dog on the head. Mr. O'Connor saw him.

"I'm afraid he misses Abigail," he said.

The hall clock ticked off the minutes. Titus thought it strange he had never noticed that clock before, but then it had never been as quiet in the house. Mr. O'Connor led the way to the drawing room.

"Can I get you something to drink—coffee, tea?"

"No, thank you," Titus said as they sat down across from the crackling fire in the hearth. He watched Barnabas circle a couple of times and finally lay at Mr. O'Connor's feet. No doubt the two of them had become fast friends in the lonely house.

A knot swelled in Titus's throat, making it hard for him to swallow. He prayed again for strength. He wanted to get some things out of the way before Mr. O'Connor said anything. "Eliza was right," he said, practically rubbing a hole through his hat. He looked up at Mr. O'Connor, who was staring at him intently.

"Go on."

"I originally came here to get even. I held you responsible for my pa's financial problems and ultimately his death." There. He'd said what had been festering inside him for all these months.

"I know," Mr. O'Connor said in a slight whisper.

Titus was puzzled. "You did? How?"

"It was all over your face when I saw you at the mercantile that day. When I asked you to be our chauffeur, I could almost see you forming a plan."

Titus hung his head.

"That's the reason I asked you to come to work for me. I had prayed the Lord would give me some way to help you and your family."

"Even though you knew I wanted to hurt you?"

"I had hurt you."

"But you didn't do it intentionally."

"No, but you thought I did." Mr. O'Connor shifted in his chair. "I know you had changed your mind before Eliza shared her bit of news. So what changed it?"

Mr. O'Connor listened intently while Titus explained about reading the letter in his box in the sitting room. When Titus finished, Mr. O'Connor heaved a sigh. "To tell you the truth, I'm glad this whole thing happened, though I don't know where it will lead. I've lived with this all these years, and I wanted to tell my wife." He rubbed his jaw and stared into the fireplace. "I thought I was protecting her."

"Like I wanted to protect Ma and Jenny from what I thought you had done to our family."

"Well, something like that," Mr. O'Connor replied. "When I came to the Lord, I should have told Lavina the truth about Abigail. I should have trusted our faith was strong enough to keep us together. Now she'll struggle with trusting me because I kept something from her." He looked at his callused hands as if seeing something there. "It's best to talk things out. Let the people you love know how you feel about them." Mr. O'Connor looked at Titus in such a way, he felt there was a hidden message in the words.

Titus nodded. Just then Barnabas's top lip curled, baring his teeth. A low growl sounded deep in his throat, then rolled forth into a full fit of barking. Suddenly the clatter of horses and a carriage sounded outside.

"I can't imagine two callers in one day," Mr. O'Connor said as he strode toward the door. Titus decided he had better leave since company was coming. He pulled on his hat and stepped just behind Mr. O'Connor as the man opened the door. In the doorway stood three women. Lavina O'Connor's face, at the sight of her husband, revealed her surprise at his shrunken appearance.

"Hello, Thomas," Lavina O'Connor said.

He stared at her, speechless.

"Aren't you going to let us in?" she asked.

Titus watched as Lavina, Abigail, and Eliza O'Connor entered the room.

nineteen

Once they entered the room, Mrs. O'Connor turned to Titus. "You might as well join us," she said. "We all need to talk things out."

Titus gulped, not at all sure he was ready for this. Still, he obediently followed the others. Once they settled in their chairs in the drawing room, Mrs. O'Connor took a deep breath as if to begin, but Eliza jumped in.

"Before you say anything, I want to apologize to everyone in this room. I brought this whole mess about, and I'm deeply sorry. I've explained everything to Abigail and Aunt Lavina, and I want you to know I'm truly sorry, Uncle Thomas. . .and Titus." She averted her gaze from Titus.

Mr. O'Connor shook his head. "No, it's not your fault, Eliza. I should have been up-front with my dear Lavina from the beginning." He looked at his wife, and she at him. His eyes seemed to beg understanding. "I never meant to hurt you. I thought I was protecting you from the pain of my sin."

A single tear spilled onto Mrs. O'Connor's right cheek, trailed off her chin, and dropped into her lap. She lowered her eyes and nodded.

Mr. O'Connor stood and walked over to her. He knelt at her feet. "I would never hurt you for anything. I was young and stupid and very. . .drunk." He buried his head against the folds of her dress.

Titus wanted to look away, to leave. The moment between the O'Connors seemed far too intimate for his presence.

"Oh, Thomas," Mrs. O'Connor cried, laying her face next to the back of his head.

Both were crying now. Titus was moved by their affection and forgiveness toward one another. Tears streamed

156

down Abigail's face. Eliza wiped her damp cheeks and shifted uncomfortably in her seat. Titus choked back his own emotions.

Mrs. O'Connor lifted her head. She stroked Mr. O'Connor's hair. "We'll talk later, dear." She looked at the others. A smile lit her face. "I just wanted you to know that during the few weeks I've been gone, the Lord has spoken to me through my friend. As you know, she lost her husband about six months ago. She reminded me how foolish it would be to let pride keep me from the man I love."

Mr. O'Connor looked up, and she smiled at him. "Every day is a gift, and we must not waste it." He offered her a weak smile, then reached over and kissed her hand. His face was wet with tears.

She dabbed at her face and looked from Eliza to Titus. "Whatever your motives for doing what you did, it doesn't matter. Hopefully, you have learned from it and will come out better people for the experience. I know I have, though it's not been an easy lesson." She patted her husband's hand.

"I want to apologize." Every eye turned to Titus.

"You know my bent on revenge. I was angry with you, my pa, and the Lord." He said the last phrase in almost a whisper. He studied his hands. "I wanted someone to pay for the pain I was feeling—"

"But you didn't want any part of this. You tried to stop me," Eliza cut in.

Titus looked at her. He glanced over at Abigail, whose face held no condemnation, only compassion. At that moment, he realized Eliza must have explained the situation to Abigail.

"I never meant to hurt you," he said, his eyes never leaving Abigail's face. Then he turned to Mr. and Mrs. O'Connor. "Or you." He ran fingers through his hair. "And you're right, Mrs. O'Connor, I've learned a lot. I'm sorry I had to learn it at your expense."

"No, Titus, the Lord has helped us all through this. Though I'm not thankful any of it has happened, He does promise to work things together for the good of those who love Him. And I believe He has done just that." Mrs. O'Connor turned to Abigail. "After all, we have our Abigail."

Abigail got up from her chair and knelt at her mother's feet beside her father. She leaned against her mother's skirts.

"Well, I think this is a good time to pray," Mr. O'Connor announced. Sobs poked through his words. "Father, despite my sin, Thou hast restored our family. And I thank Thee." He stopped a moment to blow his nose. "We know the battle is not over. The enemy will try to discourage us in the days ahead, but we bring the matter to Thee. Remind us again and again to leave it there. I thank Thee for my dear Lavina and for her forgiveness. I cannot imagine life without her."

Mrs. O'Connor's soft voice whispered, "Lord, Thou art far more gracious and forgiving to us than we deserve. Thy love and mercy never end. For that we give Thee thanks and our deepest praise."

"Lord," Abigail continued in prayer, "I thank Thee for my mother and father and for allowing me to be a part of this blessed family. Help me to lean on Thee when I don't understand things and when I am hurt by others. Most of all, help me to forgive as Thou hast forgiven me."

The room fell silent. Titus cleared his throat. "I know Thou hast forgiven me, Lord. Please help these good folks to find it in their hearts to do the same."

Eliza's small voice squeaked through the silence. "I don't know much about talking to Thee, Lord. But. . ." She paused a moment. "I'm sorry." That was all she said.

It was enough.

Mr. O'Connor and Abigail rose to their feet. The others did the same. Titus thought the whole room seemed brighter. Sunlight spilled into the room and sparkled on the carpet. His heart felt clean. Really clean. While the others embraced in the warmth of forgiveness, he decided to slip out quietly.

Stepping into the hallway, he had just reached the door when a hand touched his shoulder. He turned to see Abigail's red face, blotched with tears. "Thank you." A smile lifted the corners of her mouth.

Titus's heart soared. Before he could say anything, Mr. O'Connor walked into the hallway. "Titus, my boy, I do hope you'll show up for work tomorrow. I've had an awful time trying to manage things on my own."

Titus looked at him in surprise.

"I know you've been working construction, but that was temporary, right?"

Titus nodded.

"Well then, what say you come back to work for me?" A wide grin spread across Mr. O'Connor's mouth. He stepped up and clasped Titus's hand in a hearty shake. Behind Mr. O'Connor stood his wife and Eliza. Everyone was smiling.

Titus grinned. "Yes, sir," he said, shaking the older man's hand with gusto. "I'll see you in the morning." Titus shrugged on his hat. His gaze locked with Abigail's. Her face turned a deeper crimson, and for the first time since they had parted, he thought perhaps there was hope for him and the lovely Abigail O'Connor.

❧

"Eliza, would you come in the sitting room a moment, please?" Abigail's mother called. Abigail looked on, wondering what was happening. "Abigail, you come join us, too."

Once the women sat down, Mother looked at Eliza. "My husband tells me you only came back to clear things up and that now you're planning to leave."

Eliza's gaze lowered.

"I had taken the liberty to show Sophia your needlepoint. She had mentioned she would love to have you help her in her shop, but at the time, I knew you didn't want to stay on here. Perhaps you would now consider that possibility?"

Eliza's head jerked up. Her eyes filled with tears. Abigail felt compassion sweep over her toward her cousin.

"Of course, you know you're welcome to live with us, should you decide to stay."

It took a full minute before Eliza finally spoke. "You'd do that for me?"

"Of course we would."

Tears plopped onto Eliza's skirts. After a moment, she lifted her head, got up, and went to her aunt, embracing her fully. "Thank you, Aunt Lavina. Thank you."

When Eliza stood, Abigail got up. "Sophia's customers will love your work. Oh, and you will love working with Sophia. She's a wonderful friend," Abigail offered.

The two young ladies exited the drawing room, chattering about their future. Abigail felt as if she really did have a sister.

~

The next morning after the worship service, Abigail stepped through the church doors and into the spring sunshine. She shielded her eyes from the sun's glare and looked toward Jenny and Mrs. Matthews. She noticed Titus stood in the distance talking with some menfolk. Abigail's heart felt light and carefree like a summer lark. She edged her way through the tiny crowd toward her friends.

"Good morning, Mrs. Matthews. Jenny."

"Hello," they answered in unison.

"Are you keeping up with your studies, Jenny?"

The little girl sat in the wagon. She nodded, setting her blond curls to bouncing.

"Good," Abigail said with a smile.

Mrs. Matthews hadn't climbed into the wagon yet. She grabbed Abigail's hands. "I know it's not my place to say, child, but Titus told me what's happened with your family and all. I want you to know I'm so happy how the Lord has worked through the situation and seen you through." She patted Abigail's hand. Without a thought, Abigail gave Mrs. Matthews a slight peck on the cheek, surprising them both.

The kindness and appreciation on the older woman's face assured Abigail of the woman's genuine love for the O'Connor family. She whispered in Abigail's ear, "I'm praying for you. . . and my son." Then, as if she shouldn't have said anything, she quickly clasped her hands to her mouth.

Abigail smiled. "Thank you, Mrs. Matthews. For everything." Abigail hugged the older woman, said good-bye to Jenny, and headed back to her family's carriage. They still lingered in conversation with friends on the church grounds. As Abigail lifted her skirts to cross the yard, someone tapped her shoulder from behind. She turned to face Titus.

"Hi," he said, as if he didn't know what else to say.

"Hi." She smiled to encourage him.

"Guess you know how sorry I am." His fingers walked around the rim of his hat.

"I know."

"Um, can we start over?"

"Start over as in. . . ?"

"As in. . ." He fumbled for words.

"As in how about you come to our house for dinner tomorrow night? Then after dinner, I can beat you at checkers again."

His face brightened. "I accept." An enormous smile spread across his face, causing Abigail's heart to flutter.

"Tomorrow then."

"Tomorrow."

Feeling like a feather floating on the wind, Abigail turned toward her carriage, when she noticed Sophia catch herself and grab her stomach. Clayton ran to her side. Before Abigail could get to her, a small crowd had gathered.

An older woman turned a worried face to Abigail. "Looks like the little one is coming early."

❧

Though there was little Abigail could do, she felt grateful Clayton had let her come to their home. Mrs. Baird, Mr. and Mrs. Hill, and Sophia's mother prepared food for the little family, and Abigail saw to it that the coffee stayed fresh. Titus came along to keep Clayton from gnawing on his fingernails, and the doctor stayed busy with Sophia.

The hours dragged on, and everyone grew weary. No one

dared speak it, but concern lined everyone's brow. Sophia's cries from the bedroom filled the air with tension. Mr. and Mrs. Hill stepped outside for some fresh air. The rocking chair creaked as Angelica Martone, Sophia's mother, rocked back and forth, back and forth. Mrs. Baird worked feverishly on her needlework, while Clayton paced. He was as fidgety as a turkey just before Thanksgiving. Abigail wished she could help, but only Baby Hill's entrance into this world would make things better. Titus sat on the edge of the sofa and cracked his knuckles.

Just when the waiting seemed almost unbearable, a baby's wail called from the bedroom, notifying the little gathering that the blessed event had taken place. Clayton stopped in his tracks. It took a full minute for the idea to sink in. Pretty soon, a huge grin spread across his face, and he couldn't get to the bedroom fast enough. Everyone laughed as they watched him stumble across the room to see his wife and baby. After a few moments of suspense, Clayton burst through the bedroom door and made the announcement.

"He's a boy!"

twenty

The evening hour was upon them by the time Eli Clayton Hill entered the world. The room that had been tense with waiting now filled with tears of joy, hugs, and congratulations.

Once Sophia's room cleared out, Abigail slipped into the bedroom to congratulate her friend. She edged closer to the bed and looked upon Sophia holding her baby son in her arms. With disheveled hair and a weak smile, Sophia lifted weary but joyous eyes to her friend. "Isn't he beautiful?" she asked, looking again at her son.

"That he is," Abigail agreed. She stepped a little closer and looked down at the pink, wrinkled skin of baby Eli. With eyes squeezed tightly closed, his arm flailed about until his fist finally came to rest against his tiny mouth, and he began to suck on it.

Sophia and Abigail laughed. "He must be hungry already," said Sophia. She pulled the folds of the soft yellow blanket down around his chin and stroked her finger gently against his face. He turned his head toward her finger.

"Well, I'll leave you two to get acquainted," Abigail said, turning for the door.

"Oh, Abigail, would you ask Titus something for me?"

Abigail turned and nodded.

"Though Eliza will be doing needlework for me, I will need another seamstress to help with my business, especially now with the baby here. Would you ask him to ask his mother if she would be interested in sewing for me? She could work from her home, of course."

"Oh, how wonderful, Sophia!" Abigail said excitedly. "I'm sure she will be interested. She's wanted a job for some time but couldn't leave Jenny."

Sophia nodded. "I knew that. I've also heard people at church talk about what a good seamstress she is. It will be a real blessing to me if she accepts."

"I'll ask him tonight and let you know right away."

Sophia nodded and smiled. "Thank you," she said, her attention quickly turning back to her son.

"I love you, dear friend," Abigail whispered as she left the room.

"You ready to go home?" Titus asked Abigail when she stepped into the living room.

She nodded. "Just let me get my cloak." She grabbed her things, and they said their good-byes. Stepping into the cool night air, Abigail pulled her cloak tighter around her. Twinkling stars dotted the velvet sky while the moon hung barely a whisper above a cluster of trees. A shiver went through Abigail, but she knew it wasn't from the cold. It seemed a perfect night. Like her upside-down world had turned upright again. They stopped in front of the wagon, and Titus helped her up. He walked around and stepped up to the seat. She took a contented breath.

Titus turned to her. She could see his smile in the moonlight. "It is a good day, isn't it?"

She smiled back and nodded. Titus prompted the team into a steady trot. For the next few minutes, she explained Sophia's offer to his mother. Seeing God's hand in the matter, they talked excitedly of God's mercy and provision in times of need.

When they settled into a comfortable silence, Abigail thought about the baby. After witnessing the miracle of a newborn baby, she couldn't help but wonder how a mother could leave her child on the doorstep of another. Did she just want to be rid of a burden? What kind of woman could do that? A harsh, uncaring, cold mother.

Her mother.

A chill surged through her, but it was different from before. She pulled her cloak up tighter. The wind had chased the beauty of the night into the dark woods. An occasional blackbird flapped heavy wings against the night sky. A hoot owl cried out in the distance. The air grew cold. A lonely kind of cold. The kind of cold that made you long for the warmth of another. Her mother had died. No one knew the details. Abigail knew only that by the time she had turned three years old, her mother was gone. Her father had told her that much.

"Are you all right?" Titus asked, interrupting her thoughts.

"Oh, um, yes, I'm fine." She could feel him looking at her. She turned to him. "I can't help but wonder how a mother could abandon her child," she said, surprising herself at the intimacy of her statement.

The rhythmic *clip-clop* of horses' hooves echoed around them as the comment hovered in the air. Titus looked at her.

"I mean, didn't she care at all?" She wished she hadn't asked the question the minute it left her. After all, she knew her mother didn't care, or she wouldn't have abandoned Abigail. Still, Abigail wondered who this mystery woman was, what she looked like, what would make her do such a cruel thing.

"It is hard to understand." He grabbed her hand. "But your mother was good to you, Abigail. She gave you to the people she knew would love you most."

Abigail swallowed the tears that threatened. She hadn't thought of that before. Somehow, it made her feel better to think her mother had shown a hint of caring by leaving Abigail with her real father and his wife. And how thankful Abigail was for that! She couldn't wish for a better mother than Lavina O'Connor. "Thank you, Titus."

"For what?"

"For reminding me how blessed I am."

He smiled. "No, I'm the one who is blessed."

She studied him. "And how is that?"

He pulled the horses to the edge of the country road and turned to her. "Because you have forgiven me."

She felt her face grow warm.

Titus grabbed her hands. "I don't know if I dare presume further, but I can't wait another moment."

Abigail heard the seriousness in his voice and looked up at him. "Titus, what is it?"

"Abigail O'Connor, I have loved you from the moment I saw you in the mercantile. I tried to convince myself it wasn't so, but I couldn't deny it. With all that's happened, I don't know if you could ever feel for me—"

Abigail reached up and pressed her gloved hand against his lips. "I feel the same."

He stared at her in disbelief. "You do?"

She pulled her hand away, nodded, and smiled.

Scooting closer to her on the seat, Titus reached one arm around her back and with his other arm pulled her to him. Beneath the twinkling stars, his lips pressed soft and moist against her own, his arms slowly pulling her tighter against him. Dizziness enveloped Abigail. White lights sparked behind her eyelids as she melted into the kiss. A distant train whistle blew softly into the night air, while Abigail O'Connor prayed the moment would never end.

❧

After dropping Abigail off at her home, Titus warred with himself all the way to his house. He wanted to ask Abigail to marry him, but how could he? Being the family chauffeur could hardly appeal to a woman. No, he needed a good job that would provide for a family. But good jobs were hard to come by. He pondered the matter over and over in his mind.

By the time he got the horses unhitched and put in the barn, he was worn out with thinking. His ma and Jenny were asleep when he slipped quietly into the house. His mind continued to work the matter over as he shrugged out of his clothes and pulled on his night clothes. One thing he knew for sure: When he went to the O'Connors' in the morning, he would let them know he needed to get a different job. With that decision made, Titus climbed into bed and went straight to sleep.

⁂

The next morning, Titus had barely stepped into the barn when Thomas O'Connor came out to meet him. "Titus, could you come into the house and meet me in my study, please?"

"Sure, Mr. O'Connor," Titus said, tethering his horse to a nearby post.

Fear tugged at Titus as he took steps toward the house. Perhaps Abigail had told her parents what had happened last night and they didn't approve. What then? Would he have to give her up again? No, he couldn't do that. But neither would he want to cause strife between Abigail and her parents. His stomach churned. Abigail let him in. Her smile chased away his fear for the moment, but as soon as he entered the study and saw Mr. O'Connor, the fear returned sevenfold.

"Close the door behind you, Titus, and have a seat," Mr. O'Connor said, pointing to a chair.

The leather chair squeaked beneath Titus as he sat down. He swallowed hard and looked at Mr. O'Connor.

"Now, Titus, I want you to know we've appreciated having you help us out these past months as our driver, and you can continue on if you would like, but. . ."

Titus could feel sweat forming on the back of his neck. *Here it comes. The speech about leaving his daughter alone.*

"What I'd really like to do is get you to work at the railroad."

Titus almost choked. "What?"

"I haven't said anything before now because there just wasn't a position available. But someone has recently moved on, and I'd like to see you get the job. You'd have to be trained, of course. It would be good pay, I can assure you. Enough to set aside a handsome sum for medical school, I would imagine."

Titus's jaw dropped. Mr. O'Connor laughed. "I can see I've caught you by surprise. You don't have to decide right now if you'd rather not, but just let me know—"

"Oh, I can tell you right now. I accept!"

The two men chatted on about the job vacancy and what

Titus's duties would entail. Finally, after mustering the courage, Titus asked Mr. O'Connor for permission to marry his daughter. The older man didn't seem at all surprised, and after giving the appropriate fatherly speech, he gave his full blessing.

With those matters behind them, they left the sitting room. Mr. O'Connor took Titus into the drawing room, where Abigail, Eliza, and Mrs. O'Connor sat in front of the fireplace.

"Well, ladies, I have an announcement to make," Mr. O'Connor proclaimed.

They all looked at him. "Mr. Matthews, here, has agreed to take a position with me at the railroad."

Mrs. O'Connor clasped her hands together in glee. Abigail and Eliza shared a knowing smile. They all jumped up to congratulate him. When the commotion finally died down, Mrs. O'Connor got tea for everyone, and they sat down together.

"You see, Titus, that has been Thomas's plan all along. To get you in the railroad, I mean. He just had to wait for the opening to present itself." She smiled and took a drink of tea.

"You brought me here to work for you with that in mind?" Titus asked, amazed at God's goodness.

Mr. O'Connor smiled and nodded. "I knew the other man was leaving but wasn't sure how soon, so I had to bide my time."

The next hour was spent with excited chatter over the news. When Titus caught Abigail's look, he thought she appeared almost sad. Why wouldn't she be happy for him? He finally said he needed to go outside. He got up and noticed Abigail a little ways behind him. She followed him to the door.

"I left something in the wagon; I need to get it out," she said as she stepped through the door just behind him. They walked out to the barn together. She reached into the wagon and pulled a book from the seat. Starting to turn, Titus grabbed her arm.

"Are you upset?"

Tears sprang to her eyes.

"Abigail, what is it?"

"I'll miss you," she said in a weak voice.

He threw back his head and laughed.

"Well, I don't think it's so funny," she said, her nose pointing heavenward.

He placed his hands on her arms. "No, you don't understand. I thought something else was going on. You had me worried."

She looked at him, puzzled.

"Look, Abigail." He glanced around the barn. "This is hardly the place I wanted to do this, but I don't think I can wait a moment longer. I feel as though I could burst."

"What is it?"

"I want to marry you, Abigail O'Connor. I didn't know how I could ask you on a chauffeur's salary, but your father's offer has made everything possible. Ma has agreed to work for Sophia, so I don't have to worry about her being cared for." He stopped and took a breath. A look of apprehension settled upon him. "That is, if you'll have me." His fingers lifted her chin until their eyes met. "Abigail O'Connor, will you marry me?"

She gasped. "Oh yes! Titus, I will marry you!" Before she could take another breath, he scooped her tiny frame up into his arms and swung her around several times.

They finally stopped to catch a breath. With a gentle touch, Titus's arms encircled her as he pulled her to him. "Abigail, I've never been this happy in my life. I couldn't have dreamed you'd be the one. Yet God knew." He brushed a red curl from her eye. "The tiny baby in the basket was no secret to Him at all."

Abigail smiled up at him.

"I love you, Abigail O'Connor." He leaned toward her, his lips caressing her own with a passion that said she belonged to him.

When she pulled away, she looked into his eyes. "I love you, Titus Matthews."

She snuggled into him, and in the quiet of that moment, their declaration of love mingled with the morning air and lifted on the breeze toward heaven.

A Letter To Our Readers

Dear Reader:

In order that we might better contribute to your reading enjoyment, we would appreciate your taking a few minutes to respond to the following questions. We welcome your comments and read each form and letter we receive. When completed, please return to the following:

Fiction Editor
Heartsong Presents
PO Box 719
Uhrichsville, Ohio 44683

1. Did you enjoy reading *Basket of Secrets* by Diann Hunt?
   ❏ Very much! I would like to see more books by this author!
   ❏ Moderately. I would have enjoyed it more if

   _____

   _____

   _____

2. Are you a member of **Heartsong Presents**? ❏ Yes ❏ No
   If no, where did you purchase this book? _____

   _____

3. How would you rate, on a scale from 1 (poor) to 5 (superior), the cover design? _____

4. On a scale from 1 (poor) to 10 (superior), please rate the following elements.

   ____ Heroine   ____ Plot
   ____ Hero   ____ Inspirational theme
   ____ Setting   ____ Secondary characters

5. These characters were special because?_____

_____

_____

6. How has this book inspired your life?_____

_____

_____

7. What settings would you like to see covered in future
   Heartsong Presents books? _____

_____

_____

8. What are some inspirational themes you would like to see
   treated in future books? _____

_____

_____

9. Would you be interested in reading other **Heartsong
   Presents** titles? ❏ Yes ❏ No

10. Please check your age range:
    ❏ Under 18   ❏ 18-24
    ❏ 25-34   ❏ 35-45
    ❏ 46-55   ❏ Over 55

Name_____

Occupation _____

Address _____

City_____ State_____ Zip_____

The STUFF OF LOVE

4 stories in 1

In four interwoven novellas set in 1941, an American OSS officer enlists a mother and daughter in America and two of their relatives in Europe to carry out a clever plan.

The southern California mother/daughter team of Cathy Marie Hake and Kelly Eileen Hake combine their writing and research with authors Sally Laity and Dianna Crawford of northern California.

Historical, paperback, 352 pages, 5 ³/₁₆" x 8"

Heartsong

HEARTSONG PRESENTS TITLES AVAILABLE NOW:

(If ordering from this page, please remember to include it with the order form.)

HEARTSONG ♥ PRESENTS

Love Stories Are Rated G!

That's for godly, gratifying, and of course, great! If you love a thrilling love story but don't appreciate the sordidness of some popular paperback romances, **Heartsong Presents** is for you. In fact, **Heartsong Presents** is the premiere inspirational romance book club featuring love stories where Christian faith is the primary ingredient in a marriage relationship.

Sign up today to receive your first set of four, never-before-published Christian romances. Send no money now; you will receive a bill with the first shipment. You may cancel at any time without obligation, and if you aren't completely satisfied with any selection, you may return the books for an immediate refund!

Imagine. . .four new romances every four weeks—two historical, two contemporary—with men and women like you who long to meet the one God has chosen as the love of their lives. . .all for the low price of $10.99 postpaid.

To join, simply complete the coupon below and mail to the address provided. **Heartsong Presents** romances are rated G for another reason: They'll arrive Godspeed!